THE ONE MARVELOUS THING

Library of Congress Cataloging-in-Publication Data

Ducornet, Rikki, 1943-
The one marvelous thing / Rikki Ducornet ; profusely illustrated by
Tom Motley. -- 1st ed.
    p. cm.
ISBN 978-1-56478-519-0 (pbk. : acid-free paper)
I. Motley, Tom. II. Title.
PS3554.U279O54 2008
813'.54--dc22

                    2008014617

Stories in this collection have appeared in: *Conjunctions*—"Divorce," "Guilia on Her Knees," "The Doorman's Swellage," "The Author in Estonia," "Koi 1," "Mimi Ungerer and Janet," "The Ominous Philologist," "Panna Cotta," "Green Air," "The Parrot's Spanish," and "A Secret Life"; *Agni*—"The Wild Child"; *Bomb*—"The One Marvelous Thing"; *Fairy Tale Review*—"Blue Funk"; *Text:Ur*—"The Scouring"; *As You Were Saying*—"La Goulue in Retirement"; *Paraspheres*—"Who's There?" and "Lettuce"; *Fence*—"Ziti Motlog"; *New Orleans Review*—"Koi 2," "A Suicide," and "Thumbtacks"; *Tin House*—"The Dickmare"; the comic version of "Clean"—the *Review of Contemporary Fiction*, *Shorts*, *Ur-Vox*, and as a minicomic; and the stories in "The Butcher's Comics" were first published (sans drawings) in *The Complete Butcher's Tales* (Dalkey Archive Press).

Partially funded by a grant from the Illinois Arts Council, a state agency, and by the University of Illinois at Urbana-Champaign

www.dalkeyarchive.com

Printed on permanent/durable acid-free paper and bound
in the United States of America

THE ONE MARVELOUS THING
RIKKI DUCORNET

Decorated by T. Motley

Dalkey Archive Press 🔲 *Champaign and London*

This book is for Jean-Yves and Kimberly,
much beloved and fabulous creatures full of grace.

8 The Wild Child

14 Green Air

20 The Doorman's Swellage

26 The Author in Estonia

30 Koi

36 Painter

37 Poet

38 She Thinks Dots

42 Thumbtacks

44 Koi

48 Giulia on Her Knees

54 Mimi Ungerer and Janet

61 Ziti Motlog

65 The One Marvelous Thing

72 A Suicide

74 Divorce

78 Panna Cotta

87 A Secret life

97 The Ominous Philologist

100 The Dickmare

106 Blue Funk

110 Who's There?

112 The Scouring

117 La Goulue in Retirement

123 Lettuce

126 Oops!

128 Because His Youth Or The Parrot's Spanish

134 Chi Gong

137 The Butcher's Comics

The Wild Child

In those years when I bounded about on all fours and on my elbows fled those I feared; when, in those lucent days I scaled trees fast as a cat and sailed the treetops as the squirrels do, spreading their wings of fur and flesh, I was, I assure you, a better creature for all that, my desires both innocent and private, and what's more, easily assuaged. When I thirsted for blood, I killed a thing, a rabbit, say, a squirrel seized sleeping in its nest, a green snake, a rat fat from the leavings in the fields. There were none to balk, none to scold me, no one there to hide her face in dismay beneath her apron's ample hem. I had seen plenty of bats and frogs but never a priest, nor had I heard the words *nun*, or *needle* or *butter* and *bread*—although they say I must have been acquainted with human speech because I was quick to learn a thing or two and this despite my ferocious attempts to stop them, to stop their constant jabbering. Like crowds of crows they were, blackening the mind with their needling and nagging until I could no longer bear it. In order to taste the food they denied me for days in their righteous need to have me tamed, I—although their porridge and chops were like dead leaves in my mouth and their drear puddings, plaster (I'd have preferred a fistful of fur or last winter's bone black with frost and green with neglect)—I cried out from the cellar and up through the floor boards as best I could:

I repent!

—and this between my pretty clenched teeth. For, yes: in those days my teeth *were* pretty, and people would pay to see them, stealing a look when my patron, my master, would slide his fingers into my mouth to peel the lips way back. What fine teeth the Wild Girl has! See the pretty blush on her gums! I'd show my tongue, seized as it was between my master's thumb and forefinger—as when in the wild one seizes frogs in their boudoirs of wet grass. If they wanted more, I'd bug out my eyes, the whites burning brighter than the sunlight in those yellow days before I was forced into the bondage of roasted meat and venomous alphabets and spelling books and needlework and hymns stinking of the frass of centipedes and roots boiled to pap!

I repent!

I cried up to them because I was hungry having for whoknowshowmanydays, chewed my boots in the fury of my banishment, the cellar darker and colder than the bunghole of a corpse. I chewed and recalled the taste of a hare's crisp ear, its liver sweet as berries. *You'll burn for sure!* They'd shouted it through the cracks as I clung to my knees to keep myself from gnawing my own fists; *The Devil's on his way right now to fetch you and set you on fire!*

I'd sipped my tears, the piss that in my banishment was the only thing that warmed me; once I yelled at them with all the fury in my heart: *Let me go back, then! Back to the woods! And I will drink squirrel blood and play with the bright beetles and bubbles in the stream. What business?* I offered, rationally—or so I thought—*is it of yours?* For you see I was not yet broken; I would not *repent.* I would not kneel as they said I must to kiss the cold brass cross as bitter as the corpse of a spider. I could see no purpose in it, nor the sense of forcing my feet into those boots, the clothes that fisted up between my legs, the baths, the bath brushes, the combings, scourings, parings: I could not see it! A needle plied over and over into the white cloth, the prayers, the supplications, the answering to a name they claimed was now mine. *What need*, I'd asked, *for a name?* When all the creatures have but one name, the same name that bounds through the air like dust motes and rain?

Marie! They'd spit at me as nails are spit from the mouth of a carpenter, Marie—Angélique Leblanc! As though to call me Mary and angel and the white could tame me and keep me safe like a lock of dead hair in a box. Hah! As if they could do that! But then in the cellar I grew hungry, see: I grew peevish. Chained like a parrot to a post I grew weary and, to tell the truth, fearful for my mind. So at last I called up to them, humble, yet loud enough to be heard:

I repent! I repent! Yes! Yes! That's it! I do! And if the little Jesus will have me, I'll marry him quick as Jack and Jill go tumble; I'll beg our Father for forgiveness, see?

They listened, their ears to the floor, and then they discussed my case. I could hear them pace, back and forth, back and forth as foxes do above the dwelling of a hare. They'd let me stew—for my own good—yes, *stew*, they whispered (my ears are very, very sharp) *in her* (ugh!) *own juices.*

Ah. So that was it. Well, I was hungry, and I'd be slavish—I no longer cared. *Prithee* I'd said, *Prithee! I'll wed Jesus, I'll let him suckle my tits, I'll grovel before his little manger as the worms grovel deep in their muddy realms; I'll polish the silver and stir the porridge and ply the needle* (like the prig you wish me to be); *I'll eat my pudding with a spoon and thank the Lord for it*—although it is meat I want, raw and smoking, the taste of it purple on my tongue. Wind me up! And I'll perform for thee like a toy of tin upon a wire. I'll dance for Jesus, poor boy! Tugging at his nasty nails that pin him to that strange tree of his as a crow is nailed to a barn wall; I'll do a jig; I'll curtsy and run about in circles in imitation of the toy monkey my patron's daughter loves to set spinning on the kitchen tiles. How I loathe those toys of hers; I see no purpose there; I see purpose only in fat marrow bones, the soft throats of mice, mice I once *throttled in a trice* (those are my patron's words). Oh, I'd eat clay over pudding any day.

I once told my patron how much I admired his little daughter's throat. How to see the blood rushing there behind the ear stirred old memories. And when he blanched I reassured him—and the child so quick to weep!—reassured them both in those dulcet tones they'd taught me: *Oh! But I have found the Lord and He has shown me another, a better way!* The way of roasted mutton and mittens and mattresses and bedroom slippers; *the way of Light and Love! Your dear child, the precious poppet, the angel, the dove! Is safe with me, fear not, Master! Fear not, my doll, my rosebud, my little mouse! See?* And lifting the bright cross from my bosom I dangled it in the sunlight before her face until she grew jolly and laughed. Then, to press my point and with the money I make showing myself to strangers—for I sit in the parlor on Wednesday to speak to pious ladies about the woods and my onceuponatime life in the trees—I leapt from my chair and running into the lane bought her sweets from the vendor who was ringing his bell and calling out: *Honey drops! Chocolate drops! Three kinds of berry drops! Bright red cherry drops!* So tightly did I clutch my coins the palm of my hand was bruised black.

Once they let me out of the cellar, I thought it best that I demonstrate my perfectibility, although, to tell the truth, I'd prefer to converse with ravens and crows than these feebleminded crones in bonnets who—should I absentmindedly snap up and swallow a fly—will fall over backwards in a dead faint.

They have decided I am no orangutan, but instead an Eskimo. Because like the savage girl I was, an Eskimo will eat her supper raw and sauced with blood. They have taken my club and replaced it with a needle, and have seen to it that my hair is free of lice. I have lost all my teeth, but if this makes me less attractive, it also assures them that I am less a savage: after all, one cannot tear into a neck with one's gums.

This is how I spend my days: sitting in a chair, boots on, stays on, hair in pins, plying my needle as a bee plies the blossom: in and out, in and out. Wind me up and I mutter all the Holy Holies you wish. I make red poppies blossom at the edge of tea napkins (my poppies are too red for the dining room); I am as tidy as the drawer full of my patron's underwear. And when on a Wednesday I am asked, I say:

Well. In the woods I ran as naked as a snake and as black as an iron cooking pot. I would eat clay and the hot red hearts of sparrows. I would sleep in deep beds of brown leaves and bracken. And I would fly through the air as a squirrel does, its wings of fur and flesh stretched out like sails. And when the moon was full I'd laugh out loud to see how fat it was! Fat as the white belly of a frog near bursting with flies!

Having said this—and it is astonishing how often they wish to hear it—I sit back and watch them shudder and shift about on their chairs, their bottoms rolling this way and that, like marbles in a boy's pocket, their eyes sparked with excitement, yes! Their eyes sparked with something like envy.

Green Air

Once prized, now she languishes in the drawer, one of many contained within a cedar chest. It stands beneath a window, shut against the day. His little dog guards it from intruders.

Exactly twelve months ago they had measured his ballroom together: 666 paces one way, 666 the other. Thriving they were then: fucking and spending. His kisses tasted like sweet tobacco, and after he gave her pleasure, her sex tasted like tobacco, too.

•

She has a matchbox in her pocket, an artifact from when she was the only one, or so she believed, to light his cigar. But now the victim of his bitter policy, she sighs all day till evening and the long night through, attempting to decipher his robber's mind, the reasons for her ritual incubation. Sleepless she has all the time in the world to recall the looks of doubt and evil that often come to crowd his eyes and for which she once made a thousand excuses.

"My love!" she recalls now with horror her persistent request, "look kindly upon me!"

Yet he remains aloof, seemingly displeased with the roasted fowl, her failed attempts at conversation, the tenacity of her affection.

In her company he boils over with impatience when he is not deadly weary. She considers that if some aspire to the realms above the moon, her husband has chosen to dwell beneath it and so shoulder that planet's shadow. Surely it is this that has corrupted his mind and darkened his mood. Yet in the whore's booths he rallies, his laughter clattering into the streets like hail. Dressed to kill he takes his ease in unknown places as she staggers under the load of his many inexplicable absences. Still she persists in her folly.

"Smile upon me, my beloved," she begs, pressing peaches upon him, the ripest fig. His eyes bright with malice, his snorted amusement frustrates her virtue. With real longing she watches his beautiful hand stroke down his beard. When for the last time he kisses her, he viciously bites her tongue. As the blood spills down her chin, he expulses her from their bed and drags her thrashing to the cedar chest although she cries out: "No! No! For I am no crone! But in the heat of youth! Even the beetles!" she shrieks, "move freely about! The insignificant snails! The tent pitchers! The camel drivers! Even the serpents make their way beneath the sun, the cool of dawn!"

•

That first night locked away, she notices how outside in the streets the hubbub decreases before ceasing altogether. Sprinkled with blood, the others in the chest are silent. Silenced their sobs, their barking tongues. The winter is a bitter one; no one recalls such cold! Catching a whiff of smoke from the merchant's coffee fires she lights a match. For an instant the world is kinder.

There in the drawer she is taught the final lesson: her nature—humble, generous and kind—does not assure interest or compassion. Her one hope: that her dreadful condition may turn out to be unforeseen luck of a kind. Something might come of it; the ways of the world are mysterious. Something . . . dare she imagine it! *Wondrous.* (This is what the little dog had said, his tail held high, his eyes like two saucers, each set with a black yolked egg. "Wait and see! Wait and see! Something wondrous will come!")

•

The drawer is the only place where it could have ended because that is where it all began. Or rather, to be more precise, where she came upon the artifacts that caused her to consider that something was going on and not only in her head, mind you! That the marriage, so new! barely begun! the prior wife's body still warm!—was a figment. And the drawer—as are all things belonging to husbands—was strictly taboo. As were his pockets holding small silver and keys: taboo! But then one day, sweetly occupied by the innocence of her own wifely tasks, the house flooded with light, she found herself propelled towards the very drawer in which she now languishes.

It was the fault of the little dog, you see, until then always so uncannily quiet, who at once began to raise a ruckus with all its throat, calling and calling out to her: "Come look at this!" Insisting, "Come! Here! Look at this!" And then it happens.

She goes to the chest, her heart thrashing, not only because what she is about to do is forbidden, but because what she is about to find will change everything.

A box of gold rings. His sharp pencils and pens. The small brass instruments with which he navigates the streets. A box of matches she pockets without thinking. And she finds some little sticks meant to keep his shirt collars stiff. (It is prodigious how in the morning he arises an old man suffering desolation of mind as though in the night he had seen first hand, perhaps even participated in, all the horror of the world, only to step into the shower, his dressing room, and so transform himself into a prince. Glad-eyed he leaves the breakfast nook with a lion's muscled ease, sweetening her mind with longing throughout the day as the sun lifts and lowers in the deepening sky.)

Ah? But what can this be? Deep in the drawer she finds two little books coming unglued and held together with string. "You've found us!" they chirrup so shrilly she is startled. "High time! High time!" Raising their covers they fly directly into her hands. And the little dog prancing on his hind legs, he, too, cries out: "High Time! High Time!" It is hard to remove the string, her hands are shaking so.

The first book, the one on top, is familiar to her. It contains the names of the ship they sailed together on their brief honeymoon, the cities they visited, Pisa, Pompeii . . . the names of hotels, a list of gardens, museums—and she recalls all those distant places where it had seemed they had been madly in love, although . . . Everything written with his thick-nibbed pen and ink as black as tar. But now the second book shudders with such eagerness beneath the first she must attend to it at once. This book contains her husband's dreams, and it thrusts and rages into her heart.

•

There are a number of dreams, any number of dreams, about E. E in the green dress is how the dream begins, E in the green dress laughing. E, the dress now pushed above her legs, above her ass and he, the dreamer, the one who is her husband, fucking E, fucking E's cunt, E's ass; E naked on a green couch in a green room—why is everything green? How can her own terrible jealousy color a dream about which she knew nothing? How can it be that this venomous air, this green air that she is forced to breathe because there is no other air, is the dream's primary color?

In the dream E says, "I'll fuck you till you weep." But it is she, the one who is betrayed, who is weeping.

•

Outside the snow is falling. She has only one match left to light and so decides to save it. Nearly dead with cold, his dreams scramble into her mind like ferrets; they will not let her be.

He fucks a woman briefly encountered, a pale woman with hazel eyes flecked with gold. Yes. How fascinating women are—she can appreciate this—in all their variety. Flecked with gold, her white forehead as smooth as the egg of an ostrich. Her breasts, too, heavy and white. A woman she recognizes as someone she had once offered a perfect cup of tea, in those days not long ago when she lived full of grace and wandered freely in rooms now impossible to reach. This woman she vividly recalls he fucks in a brothel within a maze or catacomb that extends beneath the Tower of Pisa or maybe it is Pompeii because there are ashes falling all around them. He chokes upon them. She chokes upon them.

Her husband's dreams are all fucking dreams. He fucks his own sons: the one who is lame, the club-footed son, the halting son. *Have I hurt you?* he asks in the dream. *Have I hurt you?* he insists, dreaming. But his sons do not speak. Their place in the dream belongs to silence.

A year unfolds reduced to letters of the alphabet and the colors of things dreamed: black ashes, a white body, the green weather within a room. In the final entry he is fucked by someone terrifying; he has no idea who. Without color or letter she is a shadow as filthy as death, and collapses heavily upon him. *A shroud?* he wonders. Has he been fucking beneath the shadow of death all along? Could it be that simple?

•

The cold is too intense to bear and she is forced to light her last match. Its heat and clarity offer her a moment of hope at once snapped up and swallowed. Hugging her knees she falls into a dream of her own, a dream that like all her dreams these days comes to her like a malefic visitation from some lethal galaxy.

In her dream they are standing together by the side of a country road, one somehow familiar. A movie screen has been set up in a ditch and E, the E of the green dress, stands behind a projector showing a snuff film. The images smear the screen like a filthy water.

She wants to turn away, but he forces her to look, holding her wrists behind her back as when inexplicably his lovemaking had become cruel. Her head and eyes, too, are immobilized so that she cannot look away, will forever be forced to see what he could not help but see, all those things he saw night after night in those terrible dreams of his.

Outside in the winter streets people come and go on their way home with wheels of yellow cheese and fruit of all colors imported from distant places. She hears the sounds of the fruit vendors calling, and overwhelmed with longing imagines what it would be like to bite into a red fruit, freshly picked and brimming with juice.

It comes to her that if leprosy is rampant in the region, it is because the gods in their legions are unquenchable.

The Doorman's Swellage

for L.H.

ood day, sir! Looking out upon the street, I could not help but notice your interest in The Perlmutter Building. The noon is hot above and the air a plague of flies. Seeing you so well turned out, I take the liberty—one of the real pleasures of my profession—to call out to you. Please step in! Note that I do not open The Perlmutter's portals for all and Sundry.

Well, then! Allow me to introduce you to The Perlmutter. Note the generous use of morganite in the lobby and the luminous lamp dish overhead. She is the only building of her type and class in the city, and she has just been revived and refit. But if you hope to move in, I regret to say there is nothing on hand, although a current occupant—the wondrous Mrs. Gastroform—is very, very old. Should The Perlmutter quicken your interest, I would be pleased to appease you of her departure and give you a tinkle—care for a mint?—although the waiting list is long. However, between us, sir, I'll do my part to put you *right on top*! Make no bones about it, sir. My pleasure, sir! I know a gentleman when I see one. No small thing these days when all and Sunday are out and about in their birthday suits engaging in who knows what low type of nonfeasance! *O Tempura! O s'mores*! Please let me relieve you of your muffler and your hat. No? As you wish, sir!

Aha! A rotogravure has caught your eye! It is—you've guessed it—The Perlmutter in her heyday, taken by Rotifer Nubbin in 1892. *All* the rotogravures in the lobby are Nubbinses. Look at them and see The Perlmutter inside and out: everything *and* her kitchen sinks! All sixty-six of them. Now then, sir: follow me.

Here in the hallway: more Rotifer Nubbinses. This series is of the Hum Tollog suite, named for Perlmutter's mother who lived here until she died of an overlapsed pessary. (She was said to hide out in the funk hole on less than happy days.) This Rotogravure shows The Rookery, no longer extant, with its forty-four roods and perches; this is The Mew. Don't ask me what Perlmutter kept there; he kept dames in droves—but not at the same time. Here's your parlor and here's your pokery; The Ambuscade and Chummery are long since gone. That brass head is 'Old Camel Dung'—Perlmutter's mother. (In this house the weaker sex was not always honorably regarded.)

After you, sir. This room's called The Mummery. Note how each object—rotogravure, paperweight, *millefolle* and statuette possess the magic power to awaken dormant sensations; they stimulate curiosity and so: *conversation*. Before you responded to my invitation, The Perlmutter was asleep, her splendors submerged in shadows and the gloom of absolute silence. My mood, too, was melancholy. Conversation has this ideal property: it alters our moods. One is gravity-bound and then a conversation begins and provides buoyancy! But I simplify! I abbreviate! Life is full of apprehensions. You, sir, I can tell, are of a sturdy humor. A mint? I order them from Rhodes. Muscatel? A sugar drink? No? Well, then: follow me. Notice the gay Turkey carpet in the hall. We're walking on dragons. See: those squiggles there.

After you, sir: take a left. And prepare to be surprised! *This*, sir, *is The Swellage*—splendid, eh? The only one in the metropolis. It was conceived and executed by Mathew Mutterer, including the mortar boards and the table ends—all *du jus*! Note the bindings—I'll bet you are a bibliolater! I always know a bibliolater! Check out the compulsory moleskin. Stroke it, sir! Go on: *cheer yourself*! All stamped with gold *floor de leech*! And the leathers: sofa, elbowchair, grampus, *footoil*, the tripod and squab—all designed by Mutterer for Perlmutter's mother, and all *de le pope*! (If you wish, sir, remove that muffler and your hat and try out the *footoil*. Rest those oars! No? As you wish, sir! A munchie? Neither.) Moving along!

That big potted plant—*watch your head*!—is a *vagus hippopotamic* and as old as The Perlmutter herself. Don't touch it, sir! Harsh desert forage; its thorns are full of brine. It was shipped all the way from the high cliffs of Akhmar by Perlmutter's maiden mother-in-law, the philanthropod and ethnogaff: Lucy Strumpeter, whose book on nose mutilations—feel *that*!—is also bound in mole. That sappy greenness on the mantel is hers, as is the crystal dromedary, the crimp and the barometer. She was a tepid traveler.

Sometimes there's teas held here. I've seen the fingerfoods! Celery and coconut cake and stuffed olives and crab wontons—

the whole suppository! Wholesome smack, mouth watering—
although Mrs. Gastroform's small pug, smelling the meat, re-
jected it.

I can see that you are wondering about that spot on the carpet.
That, sir, is the very place Mr. Perlmutter bled to death, stabbed
many times over by his murderer: Mathew Mutterer. Those
bookends, *du jus*, are the Apollo Belvedere cut in two. But, hey!
I fear I've buttonholed you! I'll tell you, sir: you are one hot
conversation piece! How you've got me hammering on! Yet,
one cannot, should not, underestimate the connection between
conversation and happiness. The mind shudders to imagine itself isolated from others, doomed to silence, the tongue rotting
between the teeth from inactivity. Those? Bronze leg horns.

To tell the truth, I find solace here in The Swellage. And, sometimes, tears. See . . . sometimes just looking in on all the excitement, a sudden happiness surges through my heart and clutches
at my throat and I have to repress the urge to shout and jump
and sing. For, yes: I wear a skeleton on my sleeve. My service to
The Perlmutter is the remedy to—what? A *wife*! You've guessed
it! A wife less than a help meat, more a bitter worm in the pie.

Sir. Sometimes the Mystery of Sex is not enough to keep a
couple going. Or maybe the mystery and the sex were *always*
one-sided. Maybe I was always the only one mystified. Women
were made to attract and fascinate men, but I wonder: does it
work the other way 'round? (That ashtray is totally legitimate!
Ditto the cracker tin.) But, back to my marriage. I guess you
could say I've exchanged one old lady for another. That's my life's
paradox: home I'm shut out, and here: I've got all the keys! I'll
tell you something, though. When I married the wife, *I was an*

enthusiast. I'd greet the night with real excitement. In no time flat, excitement gave way to dejection. You see: we didn't dally much; we didn't fool around—although I'd hoped we would. *Hurry up, husband!* she'd bellow: *I've got other fish to fry.*

Here at The Perlmutter, I've had plenty of time to think things over. I've come to the conclusion that my marriage was propelled by a delusion, and dampened by my wife's cunning management of my moods. That door? That door leads to the Hot Air Baths. They are heated from Below. Perlmutter believed in promoting perspiration. He had a point. Unlike mine, his life was short and merry. It ended violently; a thing we might all aspire to. After fifty years my marriage hums like an engine that has no need of grease, no need of me. Should I complain the wife says: *Tell it to the Marines.* Marriage has taught me this: how to eat an entire meal without spilling crumbs on the floor.

There are more prestigious things I could do, perhaps. But I love The Perlmutter. She's a Grande Dame in a world of trollops and furthermore, she affords me—as she has today—verbal intercourse with strangers.

I think of myself as something of a gourmet: I accept only the best *popos*. Right now as we speak together, the air around us is disturbed. The sounds we make are elastic; like acrobats they bound about! Shadows stir, dust lifts, inertia is subverted by vibrations. Even before we have the time to appreciate what is happening, our ears have averted us to the *fact* of conversation. The vibrations, dear sir, are accompanied by . . . an emotion. You will agree with me: nothing is more marvelous than the faculty of speech. The greetings that open the door to friendship. Tell me, sir: does not the harmony of life depend upon the success or failure to converse amiably?

Sir. I can see that you are ready to be on your way. Perhaps another time I can show you the crypt. Yes—all the Perlmutters are there, except, of course, the ones who are living.

Well, then! A good day to *you*, sir! May I give you a squeeze? No? Thank you just the same. It was nice to *parsley*. Although we kept to shallow waters, I was pleased to ferry you about. May I give you a tinkle should Mrs. Gastroform call it a day?

The Author in Estonia

The author has been invited to Estonia. Always agitated on airplanes, she cannot sleep and so memorizes a number of useful words: *antikvariaat* (secondhand bookshop), *munapuder* (scrambled eggs), *silmatilgad* (eye drops).

Her translator fetches her at the airport. He is not happy to see her and does not return her carefully rehearsed greeting. The book, her book, now his book, their book, a book he devoted *three years of his life to,* has just received its first review, a mortally obnoxious review in his country's leading newspaper: *Pakkepaber.* In fact, it is not a review at all, but a *funeral oration.*

"Killed," he reports, enraged with her it seems. "*Powie*! *Kerbang*!" He roars with bitter laughter, and as they make their way in sleet to his car, slams his right fist into the palm of his left hand again and again.

The reviewer, *a cannibal*, a *lapidator*, "has put the kibosh on it. I will," he makes a face, "put the kibosh on *her*! *Pow*!" He punches a hole in the weather. "*Pow*! In the kisser!"

In her despair, the author fumbles for a discreet capsule of kavakava.

The problem, of course, is that she has no way of knowing if her book is now as dreadful as the critic claims:

"A minestrone!" he rages, hitting his forehead smartly on the green plastic steering wheel of his Russian vehicle. "Violent death!" he mutters into his beard, "is what I wish for her. My God!" he rolls his eyes weirdly, "This bitch give me such a *headache!*"

The author gazes out the window and takes in the traffic, such as it is, in Estonia.

"Well," she tries to soothe him, "there will be other—"

"Books? *Never!*"

"Reviews."

"None!" Is he really screaming at her? "Lady! Understand! It is over! How it stink!" he glowers, "in nostril!"

This is one of those many moments when she is happy to be a consistent practitioner of yoga. She breathes deeply and holds it in, thinking about the color yellow. Yellow illumes her consciousness like the spilled yolk of an egg. Fully, she exhales.

"You!" he peers at her threateningly, "asthmatical? Needing pharmaceutical?"

"No." She returns his stare with profound distrust. Those hands of his gripping the wheel are as big as salted hams. She wonders if her life is in danger. What does she know about him? Perhaps if she takes the conversation into familiar territory . . .

"Why," she risks, "did you change the book's title from *The Ricefield* to *The Agriculturalist's Lamenting Wife*? And why—I could not help but wonder—did you choose the word *agriculturalist* over *farmer*?"

"What difference?" he barks at her. "What's it to you?"

"That's rude." She says this gently. "To say that. You might say," she offers hopefully, breathing in and priding herself on her patience, "why do you ask? Or—"

"No difference!" He pounds the wheel with his fist. "Agriculturalist. Farmer. SO WHAT?" Suddenly sorrowful, he continues: "I am so loving book. Devote all heart's ache and why? Publical humiliating!" He hits his head with the heel of his hand and she considers throwing herself out into the mercy of the blizzard. "Furthermore—" he gnaws a knuckle—"the critic, she is Russian riffraff. She is," he pretends to spit, "*phtooey*! A Jew!"

Sitting as straight as a good piece of copper drainpipe she tells him: "As was my father. My father," she repeats, "was a Russian Jew."

She has stunned him. With loathing she watches as from under his fur collar, his blood boils up to his ears and his cheeks. Even the whites of his eyes turn pink.

"You . . ." he says at last, nearly choking, "This . . . have cut out my tongue. Cut out and—" is he gazing at her tearfully? "Put on plate!"

In silence, in terrible weather, he drives her to her hotel, a surprising place of opulent decrepitude. She takes a bath in blessedly hot water in a tub shaped like a shoe with feet, and after a nap eats sausage and *munapuder* alone in an oversized room sparked with cut glass chandeliers and barely animated by a very old waiter.

Over the next few days she will find the pharmacy and used bookshop, and she will stand ankle deep in snow admiring curiously crafted leather vests as stiff as upholstered armchairs. She will not see her translator again, nor will her publisher call.

When she returns to the airport, she will do so in a taxi, and charm her driver by showing off her newly acquired vocabulary—the words for pea soup, sprats and smoked flounder, and the wonderful (and, as it will prove to be, *unforgettable*) word for pickle: *hapukurk*. Her pronunciation will amuse him, and they will make merry together, and they will laugh, merrily, together.

Koi

Already dangerously overextended, the Summer Program Director is hyperventilating. The Visiting Writers have landed. Some are drunk, some stoned, and one throws fits. Subject to boils, the Creative Non Fiction Person sobs in the infirmary.

For months the S.P.D. has been daily humiliated by his chair—an inexplicable narcissist who in his briefly overrated youth nailed the only job he'd ever have—and this before he failed to live up to absolutely everyone's expectations—those of his publisher, his colleagues, students and wives. Only his children—who had come into the world without expectations—have not been disappointed. Of his promise persists his abundant hair—always an asset in failure—and a temper sharp enough to cut cheese.

In the grips of an irresistible fantasy, the Summer Program Director exhales. He inhales; despite himself, he breathes.

His Fantasy:
Perched on the chapel roof, invisible and utterly alone, he plays hackisack as the entire campus burns.

•

Merrily the dinner bell is ringing. Seeing the participants cross the lawn, the S.P.D. is overcome with sadness. He knows they are about to be treated to bad food and, starting promptly at 9 A.M., mortification. Some have acquired a habit of self abasement. Others, new to the program, will be taken down a peg and even suffer physical harm on the part of the Poets and Writers (when was that curious distinction first made and why?)—not one of whom is visible but instead enjoying a more hospitable elsewhere drinking the good local beer and gnawing ribs.

Memories of recent humiliations plague him. His new office—once a janitor's closet—is smaller than the last one. However, it has a window—a postmodern architect's version of an ox eye. As the line on the lawn snakes into the commons, he watches.

Only two brief decades earlier he had stood in a similar line balancing a tray of bologna quesadillas and weeviled beans so horrible he had complained. Such spunk he had had then! When was it that he had ceased to complain? The smell of burned gravy fills the air. *Everything*, he mutters, *is defective*. Even his own writing which he has not dared look at in years, the yellowed pages as peppered with frass as an ill-kept pantry.

He rises. He has promised the Creative Non Fiction Person that he will look in on her. To do this he must run the gauntlet of dead trustees who bear down upon him from their foaming frames. Somewhere a desperate squirrel scuttles in a deep chimney. How, he wonders, can he be expected to endure another instant?

Mild as a goat, he steps onto the path. He does not wish to be recognized and in this he is not disappointed. It irritates him that the campus appears to be constructed of thick slices of salty ham. Passing the koi pool he thinks how easy it would be to poison their water. Longing for lightning he glares at the horrible clock tower mortared in mustard and roofed in pastrami. Exhausted, his bitterness enveloping him like a mantle of dung, he does not see the poet lying face up in the path. He is sent flying, badly skinning his knees. What has happened? Unmistakably, she is dead. She smells of fish and is clenching her teeth. Like his chair, she, too, had once been vastly overestimated. In the sky a mysterious ball hovers. The S.P.D. is so agitated he does not recognize the sun. A buzz of concern brings him fully to his senses.

A surprisingly large number of participants are on cell phones, and women of various ages and conformation, their navel studs mocking him, kneel keening in the murderously green grass. The infirmary—always seriously understaffed, is close at hand and, as in a dream, the poet's body is hastened away. He relishes its absence, although painfully aware that the eighteen Anarcho-Dadaists who have signed up for her class, are closing in. In a pinch his wife can take over, although she was, or had been, in the full promise of her youth, a Neo-Formalist.

A terrible blow he lies agreeably as the poets circle him like wasps around an open bottle of vinegar. With misgiving he approves their earnest request to devote the next evening to a reading of the corpse's oeuvre which he has always mistrusted. He tells them that Malva *can fill in the gap in a pinch*—a phrase he cannot repeat to his wife over dinner without succumbing to a fit of mad laughter.

Malva is, as she is so often, furious with him.

"They're Anarcho-Dadaists," she screams, her lovely brow knotted with loathing. "They've declared a fatwa on Neo-Formalism. They'll eat me alive!"

"They're also masochists." He says this hopefully. "Tell them to go out into the country and hurl themselves into barbed wire and write about it. Tell them to hurt themselves with hammers and to write about it." For the last time he attempts to gather her into his arms. "I'm in the mood for love," he croons, attempting whimsy. "Only because you're near me."

•

The phone rings. They stand in silence as the message machine informs them in real time of a deepening crisis. The Anarcho-Dadaists are demanding the corpse for the rest of the week. After all, they have paid for it. His chair is sympathetic and he is disinclined to reimburse tuition. Already it is clear that the poet's family is not eager to claim it.

Sometime after midnight the Town Council—exceptionally convened—authorize a transfer of the body to the koi pool, now hastily emptied of water and fish, and filled with ice. At dawn photographs of the installation are taken and e-mailed to Cerebral Cortex. They are accepted for immediate publication online.

Beautiful in black lycra, Malva stands in a swarm of Anarcho-Dadaists in the hostile pose that will make her internationally notorious within the hour, and precipitate her head first into the vortex of a hip and thoroughly disagreeable crowd. She will take to wearing lizard skin pants, her unblemished forehead threaded with ball bearings, her clitoris with thorns.

It is Friday night. The last writer has been returned to the air, and the corpse, airborn also, and in Malva's care, wends its way to Munich. There it will be transmuted to plastic cubes. Malva has been asked to curate the cubes in Barcelona. The chair has flown off also, to accept a minor award in Roumania.

The Summer Program Director finds himself alone, more desperately alone than he had ever imagined or intended to be.

Painter

They have given him a spacious studio. He has six months to complete his project. He persists in working on canvas. This is considered anomalous, and so he is grateful.

The studio overlooks the previous artist's project: a series of fifty concrete ears exactly thirty feet high. Plagued by a delicate constitution, his painting is disrupted by an irrational idea that the ears are party to his mind.

He abandons his brushes and builds himself a tall ladder. He uses this to peer down into the first ear. Shouting, he precipitates a deafening echo. He suffers an imperious need to shout into each ear, and does so over the next ten days. Overwhelmed by tinnitus, he is soon incapacitated. He begins to bark. His estranged wife is flown in from Tuscaloosa to coax him down from his ladder. She deposits him in a safer place.

Poet

She is a poet, and as long as she can remember, she has been viscerally anxious. Despite her insomnia, she accepts a fellowship from the Fossil Fuel Foundation. The fellowship affords her the time she needs to write about her insomnia and its causes. Her book will be titled: The Greenhouse as Gas Chamber.

She Thinks Dots

Surrealism is in the doghouse, as is the pyramid and the triangle. She thinks dots because so many are into squares and straight lines. Everyone marvels at the persistence of cubes. Dots are powerfully feminine: think nipple, breast and cunt-hole; asshole.

Thumbtacks

My pieces are set out on eleven square acres of level land in North Dakota. Visitors, mostly Europeans hoping to catch a glimpse of Redskins, have a tendency to make cracks about my so-called *imperialist tendencies.*

"Why so many?" they ask.

"This is the Land O' Plenty, assholes," I say. "Get a grip!"

My pieces are made of stainless steel. They will persist long after the last puffin has laid the last egg. Like the politicos of this great country of ours, they are big, heavy and redundant. But, hey! America is the Land of Redundancy *par excellence*—excuse my fries.

Speaking of France, did you know that Louis XIV had a hall of mirrors in which he could see himself replicated to infinity? Walking down that hall, a short, fat, astigmatic clock-maker *knew* he was King. The Industrial Revolution, the Triumph of Capital, Global Warming, Pop Art, pop tarts—started here. And moving pictures. All the things we love.

Recently a very blonde babe from Holland called me a megalomaniac to my face.

"Listen, honey," I said. "Here anybody worth their salt is a megalomaniac. American art is all about exuberance," I told her. "Money to burn. Engorgement."

This little speech happened to turn her on, thankyouverymuch. And with the blessings of Uncle Sam, we enjoyed more than a few rounds of ring-around-the-rosie, and a not negligible number of repeat performances of ding dong dooh-dah day!

Koi

fig. 1

For thirty years, the gallery is her fiefdom. It gives her status and access to men, although—now that she has hit middle age (and the collision has left bruises)—the youngstuds are taking their stuff

fig. 2

to a rival across town. Meanwhile, her own stable boys are growing old fast.

They are bitter. Their bowels are irritable. They expect her to do more. She reminds them

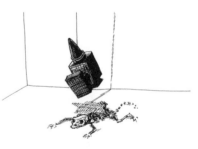

fig. 3

that the interest in art has fallen. Because of Bin Laden. The cost of organics, of home furnishings and pharmaceuticals.

Once two of her boys had made a big impression in Seattle. For two months they defined cutting edge. Tyler Zip had exhibited 120 pit bulls made out of black umbrellas, beside Crisp Banana's mountain of blue spa-

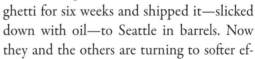

fig. 4

ghetti. Crisp had boiled spaghetti for six weeks and shipped it—slicked down with oil—to Seattle in barrels. Now they and the others are turning to softer ef-

fig. 5

fects in an attempt to loosen the local yuppies' Italian wallets. Two examples:

fig. 9

fig. 7

Jack Quicker builds coffee-table sized silicone cakes studded with plastic bonsai, and Nip Tuck upholsters discarded furniture with freeze-dried tangerines. Four weeks ago, he had papered the gallery walls with citrus peels, and nailed plastic sushi to the floor. Shrugged off by the critics, the show has only just come down. How exhausted she is!

fig. 10

fig. 11

Recently she has undergone surgery and looks younger if almost strange, as though the surgery revealed a latent gene. She wonders if there is a place—an island maybe as yet undiscovered—where people all look like this—O, it is *subtle*!—like koi.

fig. 11

fig. 14

Her boys call for loans. They smell of nicotine and tar. Her openings are undermined by their tendency to corner enthusiasts—all non-smokers—and bully them. Her rival's boys smoke kif. Good

fig. 11

stuff, flowery, exotic. *Her* openings smell of paradise and rock with laughter.

fig. 16

Looking back to Seattle with nostalgia and clearly losing touch,

fig. 18

she agrees when Tyler Zip proposes to flood the floor with pages torn from old copies of Kafka's *Metamorphosis* and, woefully na-ked, climb into a bathtub crepi-tating with centipedes. Although she keeps up with pop culture,

fig. 17

it does not occur to her that the critics might fault her for offering up a poor imitation of a wildly popular T.V. show in which men and women bed down each week with nastiness and filth.

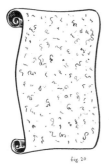

fig. 20

Opening night the gallery thrums with the whine of several million recorded mosquitoes. The artist is arrested for indecency—publicity of a kind—but she must pay to bail him out of jail. Before she knows what is happening, the city health commissioner has sent over a bri-gade dragging hoses; they chase everybody out and soak the place with poisons. At-tracted by the sound of mosquitoes, endangered bats are caught up in the fray. Their terrible bodies litter the street. She is sued by both the city and the Sierra Club.

Ruined, she is forced to sell to a beautiful Asian teenager named

fig. 21

Kiku, who quickly makes a name for herself designing exotic muffins. The muffins are baked on the premises. Kiku exhibits sexually provocative portraits of kiwi and papaya. Her scene couldn't be hotter. Should one of the stable boys wander in from habit, he is shown the door.

Giulia on Her Knees

Hiram first saw Giulia on her knees in the Ognissanti; "I've always liked," he'd later joke with his friends, "to see a pretty woman on her knees." And Giulia *had* been pretty—if a bit thick in the ankles and waist. (Her pale blonde hair was too thin.)

She was too quiet. Although it aggravated Hiram whenever she attempted a few words in public. It was her accent, he told her, that so frustrated him. Although once he had found it charming: "I like to see a pretty woman stumble over her own tongue!" What's more, she was too serviceable. "A real ox!" Although he expected her to anticipate his needs: something hot to drink, something cool. The chisels sharpened just so, the bills paid, the table set and the meal served within moments of his return to the house after a long day in the studio. The meat tender and well seasoned.

From the kitchen window Giulia monitored Hiram's moods. She was loyal. Because to create a work of art involves risk, and an uneventful domesticity allowed him to dance with his demons, the bright demons of his genius. Besides, didn't she *rule the roost*? It has been her task to erase uncertainty from his daily life. To assure a *well orchestrated household*. (As a girl she had studied the viola; often she thinks in musical terms. His voice when he calls her: *spiccato*. Her response: *con anima*!) Once when he was feeling more kindly toward her, having feasted with friends on the rabbit she had prepared, her incomparable polenta, he acknowledged that together they "played a good game. A good game of complicity." These words had reassured her. They were the evidence that things were not as bad as they seemed. She served the coffee *vivacissimo*! Hiram noticed. "What makes the ox dance?" he thundered, his laughter bouncing off the walls.

•

There is a painting by Raphael, a St. George and the Dragon in which a blonde dressed in muted scarlet kneels in the grass, praying. Giulia on her knees is like her, still and pale. Silently retreating behind the folds of a heavy velvet curtain, Hiram makes a close study of Giulia's face and body. Her eyes are fine. If her chin is too fleshy, still she is very like Da Vinci's portrait of a girl holding a weasel. And her body! Her body is lovely. Yet, like her face, it is imperfect or, rather, it is perfect because it brings to mind the thickened, somewhat clumsy bodies painted by his beloved Giotto. When she stands and turns to go, Hiram slips as gracefully as he can from the shadows and in his impoverished Italian whispers that she is *wonderfully formed*. Giulia laughs. What is this funny, charming, barrel-chested stranger trying to say? What uniform? She is wearing no uniform! Yes! Timid Giulia laughs!

Hiram takes Giulia's hand and presses it to the cold marble of a statue; he attempts to explain that this is his medium. Marble. She sees how it sparkles as if studded with grains of sand. And then they are together in the street, a familiar street, flooded with the rich, buttery light of late afternoon. And she is walking beside him. An American! Like the ones who liberated Europe! Who stood high above the crowds in their tanks and trucks, tossing *cioccolato*. The taste so powerful Giulia nearly faints in her Nonna's arms. And he is so much older than she. He could be her papa! All this emboldens her.

"I like wax better," she tells him. She is thinking of the statues of the saints. So uncannily lifelike. "Wax," she tells him, "is warmer. *WAX*," she repeats and he, because he does not understand, runs back into the church to buy candles, thick, yellow candles that fill her arms like flowers. Unable to contain her laughter—never has Giulia laughed like this!—she attempts to set him straight. "*Cera! Cera!*" And he, he thinks she wants to dine! *Cenare!* To dine! He is jubilant.

If Hiram's vocabulary is limited to the great moments in Italian art, he also knows the names of things to eat. Here they are together, at table! And Hiram orders an enormous quantity of food for them both: *zuppetta*! He shouts it; *zuppetta di cannelloni*! Tomorrow! he shouts. *Prosciutto*!

"He means *next*," she tells the waiter, "not tomorrow, but *now*!"

"With olives!" Hiram cries, "*con olive!*"

And he tells her she is *carina*; she is *caramella*—which makes her laugh even more.

"*La Fregole!*" he tells the waiter as he pours out the house wine, "*con cozze e vongoolay!*"

"*Vongole!*" she attempts to correct him. He tells her she is *carrozzina* which utterly bewilders her because it is the word for pram. She ceases to laugh and instead, blushes.

Over soup he finally manages to convey that he is *a builder of statues.* She is impressed. She asks him if his statues *seem alive,* for in her mind these are the best. *Like the ones in wax!* She tells him. Because they are almost human. *I like their eyes!* Giulia touches her own. *They look so human!* Do his statues look alive? Looking into his pocket dictionary that spills its leaves onto his knees he says no, no, alive is not his intention. *Emozione*— this is what he wishes to convey. Complex . . . what is it? *Complesso! Si! Complesso emozione.* The man of genius must invent his own forms. How can he explain this to her?

Hiram's emotions are always complex. He would worship this girl; he would lick the bones that move above her breasts and wing their way to her shoulders. He would push himself against her heavy form to quicken it. He sits back and gazes at her, watching her suck a clam from its shell, watching her tear her bread. As always when a woman interests him, he assesses her as an object in space.

"*Lapidare.*"

Giulia gazes up at Hiram. She understands that he works in stone. She tells him that, if, until this moment she has preferred wax over stone, it is because *wax is like flesh.* And the glass eyes! How she admires them. (She has never said this much to anyone.) *Ma . . .* she acknowledges. *But.* Marble lasts longer. Your statues, she tells him, *they will last forever*! *Per Sempre.* Forever. *This,* she decides, makes Hiram *straordinario.* Remarkable.

Never has she been so clever! She cannot wait to tell her sister how clever she has been. She has told a man he is *straordinario*! And he has told her an American word: *remarkable*!

Their courtship: *Bocconcini di manzo!* lasts a week. Here is a man, she tells her sister, who knows how to enjoy life's pleasures.

Giulia is nineteen. The next thing she knows she is standing over a hot stove in a small farmhouse kitchen in northern Vermont: *Vellutata*! *Tagliolini*! Grease spatters and hits the stone floor.

Now Giulia is almost sixty, and her man, the man she has struggled so desperately to both please and forgive, is failing. There had always been other women which makes it harder to be compassionate, women who, as the years passed, became younger, much younger than she. Yet she could not blame him. After all, he was a great man, a remarkable man—or so they had both thought.

Although . . . a great man would not have been abandoned by the world as he has been. The last time the people from the gallery came to see his work (Oh! That was years ago, now!) they did not stay for lunch. As they walked back to their car she overheard them talking about Hiram. They said he was stuck. They called the work dated. *Dated*!

When she had first discovered his infidelities she had shouted—she! She who had never shouted at anyone, not ever! Not even as a child! And she had sobbed. He told her she was behaving like the wife of a postman. The wife of a grocer! This she did not want to do. She learned to hold her head high at the supermarket, at the dry cleaners. She did all she could to squeeze every last drop of bile from her bitterness so that it came to resemble worldliness. She was thought to be haughty. She dressed in the eccentric threads of the successful artist's wife. She was the only woman in town to own an ikat coat and scarves made of batik. If one ate at her table, the linens were all authentic Japanese indigo. At these dinners the food was exquisite and Giulia silent. When the drinking got serious, she left the room.

Hiram has aged badly. Ill-tempered and gouty, he throws his shoes. He curses her; he curses the entire universe. These days he needs a cane. He is bitter. Old age is a personal affront, an unforgivable humiliation. And then there is that other thing that she has never allowed herself to think about, that other thing . . . Its subversive power threatens to annihilate them both. The truth. There! Na! She'll say it! She leaves her kitchen and goes out into the yard to say it! Gigantic. Too big to be moved without a great deal of fuss and bother and expense (and now nobody wants them!), Hiram's statues dwarf the yard. Gigantic and ugly! Ugly as sin! Nothing she has ever seen is uglier.

"*Brutto*!" Giulia shouts this until she can shout no more. "*Brutto*! *Brutto*!" She feels as though a swarm of bees has taken possession of her skull.

When she returns to her kitchen, Giulia gazes at her reflection in the mirror. The little mirror beside the sink where, over the years, she has hastily dabbed her lips with rouge, reddening her lips in case the remarkable man chooses to kiss them. *Why*, she wonders, *why* did she become the sort of woman who spends a lifetime on her knees scrubbing spattered grease off the floor so that some mean bastard can walk on it?

When Giulia was a child, her father told her a story she found especially fascinating. Cinyas, the hero of Cyprus, promised Agammemnon fifty boats so that he should prove victorious at Troy. But when the boats arrived they were all toys made of clay, with crews of clay. Giulia's marriage to Hiram reminds her of this story.

Mimi Ungerer and Janet

Mimi Ungerer and Janet are in their early forties, girlish, old friends, neighbors, confidantes. They are well read, sensitive, easily moved, excitable, passionate and unfaithful. Mimi Ungerer is unfaithful to Henry, and Janet is unfaithful to Vinnie.

Dizzily perched on the cusp of fame if not greatness, Mimi Ungerer is relishing her own reflection. With growing displeasure, Janet is aware how eagerly her friend is vamping, the fine bones of her face burning in the glass. She is vamping for her lover; Janet might as well be stranded on Mars. Or, perhaps, it is Mimi Ungerer whose longing has transported her to a region far beyond the world, her bedroom and its mirror.

A few days earlier, Mimi Ungerer had uncovered a number of large trunks in the attic of a newly purchased property. The trunks were brimming with clothes, everything stitched by hand and, despite their age, in perfect condition. *A trousseau!* Mimi Ungerer had breathed into the phone. *The bride . . . well, she must have died! I hope tragically.*

There is much fine embroidered cotton, and several stunning dresses in crêpe de chine. They shimmer in the early evening sun like yolk of egg. Janet cannot help but stroke them. She has always loved vivid things. But she has married a man who raises goats and sheep, and the market for wool and cheese, even very good wool and cheese, is unexceptional. These days Janet is rarely out of dungarees.

Slender, broad-shouldered and tall, Mimi Ungerer slips on an ankle length skirt and tightly waisted jacket with muttonchop sleeves. Although Janet has been told that she is beautiful, she feels fearfully plain as her friend turns this way and that. Janet thinks that Mimi Ungerer's unflagging fascination with herself miniaturizes everyone within reach. Even her lover, who feeds her dream as pellets feed the fish, is in her presence half the man he is out in the world.

"There," Mimi Ungerer says to Janet, indicating a thickly folded garment the color of suet that lies like an overturned bucketful of lime beside the sumptuous spill that singes the bed, "That one's yours."

Even before she puts it on, Janet despises it. Larded with heavy snaps, it crosses over her heart, obliterating her breasts and waist—the best things she has. It brings to mind a fencing vest or worse: a straightjacket. One artfully dyed eyebrow raised in mockery or amused affection—Janet cannot tell—Mimi Ungerer hands her the skirt.

"It's a set," she enthuses. "Linen."

The skirt, too, has snaps. Janet thinks that in ten thousand years when everything will have perished and turned to dust, the horrible "set" will surely persist.

"Fabulous," Mimi Ungerer exults as she slips into a copper-colored sheath in which her thighs glister. "I'll tell you what," she speaks into the glass, "we'll dress like this for dinner. Won't Henry and Vinnie be amused! Janet? Janet! Stop making faces! You couldn't look better!"

"But . . . *I could.*" Janet attempts as with real lust she eyes a skirt of toffee-colored tussah.

"No!" Mimi Ungerer barks decisively. "I have plans for that." And in a conspiratorial whisper: "Can you imagine? It's been four months! The bastard took his wife to Lesbos! I've been sitting on coals! But now—"

Suddenly Mimi Ungerer is naked. In the next moment, the toffee colored skirt tumbles over her limbs.

"Fetch that, Janet, will you." She points to a creamy blouse with gold green buttons that scuttle up and down the front like scarabs. For the briefest instant, Janet presses the blouse to her breasts. "The closet—" Mimi Ungerer waves Janet to it. "Grab the copper sandals, Sweetie, will you."

Fully dressed, Mimi Ungerer stands pooled in light, feral, expensive and inaccessible. "See?" she asks Janet; "see what I mean?"

"I do," says Janet coolly, "see."

Mimi Ungerer frowns. "Damn," she says to her reflection, "she really dislikes the summer suit!"

Janet thinks everything is lovely except for the horrid, horrid, "summer suit" so-called.

"I feel like I'm wrapped in stale brie," she says, getting her dander up.

"Have it your way then," Mimi Ungerer mutters, ice on her tongue. When the two friends inhale, their throats burn.

"Ah! Beauties before their glass!" Henry Ungerer's head appears drolly around the door frame. It bobs there, seemingly bodiless, buoyant and whimsical, like something sketched by Edward Lear. "How wonderful you look!" he says to Mimi. Those buttons are a blast!" Henry is a collagist and has a fated attraction to small, bright things. Often there is a feather caught to his trousers, a sequin to an elbow, a scrap of newsprint to a sleeve.

"You can't have them," says Mimi Ungerer decisively. Clowning, Henry pinches his wife's cheek.

"A real dish," he crows as his wife taps her foot impatiently. "And who are you dressing up for? Not *me*, is it? Everyone flirts with Mimi," Henry tells Janet, "but when the evening's over, I'm the one who gets to take her home!" His laughter tumbles into the room like broken crockery. "My *God*!" he exclaims, gazing at Janet with real concern, "what has she stuck you with?"

"I'm a war victim." Janet is grinning now; "beneath these bandages my body is covered with burns."

"Take it off!" Henry bellows, and at once investigates the pile. The phone rings, and Mimi hastens to it.

"Aha!" Henry triumphs, retrieving with flourishes an exquisite tea gown of pale green silk. "*This*," he says, "*is wild*. And! What have we here?" He snakes loose a long sash of darker green embroidered with goldfish. "Put it on!" he beams at her. "Look! I've turned away—"

His back to her, Henry faces the mirror. With real surprise Janet sees him searching her eyes with intensity. She tears at the snaps and tosses the thing to the floor, giving it a brief, gleeful kick. Then, as Henry looks on, she slips on the gown and, vamping in turn, wraps the sash around her waist in several slow turns.

"Sensational!" says Henry.

And Mimi Ungerer? All this time she has been murmuring into the phone. Janet and Henry share a look; both know she is speaking to her lover. When she realizes that they are aware of her again, she cries out breezily: *Yes! Yes! Next week! Bye, darling!* syrups Mimi Ungerer.

Ashen, she faces her husband and friend.

"The agency," she tells them. "They've had to cancel and re-schedule." Henry and Janet know that Mimi is too hot to be re-scheduled. Any day now she will be stellar, or nearly so, in the way her lover is stellar, so stellar one cannot take a walk downtown without bumping into one of his bronzes. He has always been stellar, or so it seems, burning through the scene like a comet. And like a comet, his tail is always on fire. Which is hard on Mimi Ungerer. Looking at her now, both Henry and Janet can see how hard. Her eyes two cysts of very dirty glass.

"Well," she says, and begins to unbutton the fabulous blouse. Henry reaches out and takes her hand in his. Perhaps if his collages were more appreciated, they could be happier.

"Do leave it on." He says this tenderly. "And let's be off, dearest. Or we shall be late for dinner. Vinnie is roasting lamb." Janet sees that his eyes are brimming with tears.

Pulling her hand from her husband's, Mimi Ungerer turns on them both.

"Yes!" she laughs bitterly. "You're right! We cannot be late for Vinnie's lamb! Vinnie's fucking god-damned lamb! But you know what? I'd rather eat my own heart skewered on a stick! Yes! My own heart and brain, roasted, do you hear me? On the fire—" Her fingers deep in the moss of her hair as if to tear it out by the roots, she dashes, as a child might, from the room.

On the stairs the copper sandals nearly fail her, but Mimi Ungerer rights herself, if not triumphantly.

Ziti Motlog

for Sunya and Mark

This story takes place in a garden. I have great affection for gardens, and this one was no exception. It was more of a backyard than a garden, but it had a number of mature crab apple trees flaunting vivid pink blossoms. Beneath the back porch light, daffodils were rioting; my hostess's young guests were beautiful and eager to get drunk.

In one corner of the porch was a large tub packed with iced beer, and in the other sat Ziti Motlog, a pleasant enough looking woman of middle age. We were introduced. Middle aged myself, I responded to her overtures, although her eyes were tearing because something or other had just moved her. She was, I discovered within moments, easily moved. "It is," she gasped good naturedly, "because of faulty plumbing. Faulty plumbing!" she repeated, dabbing her eyes with a very damp sleeve. Yet, as I would soon find out (and this despite myself, for I longed to flee), if her plumbing *ran away* with her, the cosmos was in her control. Ziti Motlog possessed a *heightened sensory awareness*; she had a direct connection with all those things that confound the rest of us: Evil, for example. Evil and its dreary wake of disheartedness, anxiety and bitter bile. If I would *indulge her*, if I would *humor her*, the world would be better for it, and I, too, would profit. If not, we'd have a good laugh and call it a day. *No problem!*

I am not a rude person, and fault myself for erring on the side of politeness. I knew I needed to bolt, yet it seemed my hostess was fond of Ziti Motlog or, at least, was grateful for her tears.

My young friend had just received her B.B.A. in Hotel Management. Her first job—a real plum—was in Bombay. Ziti Motlog feared the change would be hard on her, knew it would be hard: "Change *is* hard!" But, "It's the hard parts, the ones with gristle, the ones you've got to chew on with lots of determination and saliva," Ziti Motlog beamed tearfully, "that allow us to grow. It's all about growth," she emoted, fearful that I had not ever considered this seriously enough. She seized my hand although it would have been clear to anyone else that there was no chemistry between us. "The Tree of Life," she said, releasing my hand all too briefly and flourishing her arms as though preparing to fly off, "has roots like *this*! Do you," she yearned, her bosom leaping in its cage, "know *why*?"

I could not imagine why. Again, she grabbed my hand. I gazed at Ziti Motlog with stupid amazement, unable to act or move. Submerged in self-loathing I could not think. My discomfort thrilled Ziti Motlog who stroked my arm to soothe me. She would save me from my demons—of this she was convinced. She would radiate healing vibrations, and she would weep. The weeping had already begun.

"It's because of suffering! Suffering," said Ziti Motlog, "makes those roots and branches grow!" Again she withdrew her hand, and lifting her arms above her head, waved them about in an air that smelled of spermy youths and barbecue and marijuana. I recalled nursery school; I recalled standing among my fellows with my arms above my head. And Mrs. Mortuous, the daughter of Demeter, The Enemy of Raised Voices, urging us to wave our branches in the tangible wind of her earnest benevolence.

"The Age of Aquarius is upon us!" Ziti Motlog offered unctuously; "it is the Age of Seeds, the Seeds of Life, the Seeds of

Change. And here they are!" She dropped a handful of virtual seeds in my shrinking palm, and with deliberate tenderness, folded my fingers over them. "Do not fear!" she admonished—for I was rife with loathing—"but allow the seeds to *growgrow-grow!*" She drove this advice home by prodding the flesh of my arms with her fingernails. Revulsed, I pulled away and she, still eager to comfort me, patted my shoulder.

"Receive the seeds!" she caroled, "your world is about to change! You are about to be *a much happier person!*"

Again her eyes swelled with tears and I, I longed to bite her on the neck. How dare she think of herself as someone who could give me happiness? Moments before I had been happy enough, had blessedly forgotten the seemingly insurmountable crises that characterize our precipitously failing world. Ziti Motlog reminded me of all I hated. She was sappy, condescending, and over confident. She was ridiculous and yet she had managed to enrage me.

"Everybody wants to grow!" she pouted, ignoring my vituperous look, "and so do you! Can you *feel it?*"

"Why don't you leave me alone?" I said then.

Stunned, Ziti Motlog's eyes dried up.

"You don't want the seeds!" she marveled. "Whatever! Someone else will know their value." Deeply resentful she began to wail. "No wonder things are such a mess! I feel sorry for you," she blushed in a tremblor of temper, "so fearful of change!"

"I'm *not* fearful of change!" I cried. "Who gave you permission to mother me? I don't want your blasted seeds or your platitudes. And I don't want your god-damned tears!" I stood up, yet did not turn away, somehow mesmerized by the herring pond that was Ziti Motlog. Her girth, perhaps. Her certitudes.

"You are just like a lover I had a long time ago!" Ziti Mot-log decided surging from her chair; released it shuddered and swayed. She was monumental, dressed as a goddess in the many folds of some sort of tent.

"He stabbed me!" she stormed, "just as you have done. *Here.* In the heart. Look!" Before I could turn away she had torn apart the bodice of her dress. I saw the scar rising like a slice of raw fish laid out on a shard of ice. Ziti Motlog's scar was the inescapable proof of my fatal incapacity.

"I am the emissary of the good!" she foamed in a sea of garments. "My only purpose to inoculate the species! To pass on the seeds! *Why won't you take them*? You did this," she glowered, polishing the scar with her thumb. "*You,*" said Ziti Motlog, "*and your ilk.*"

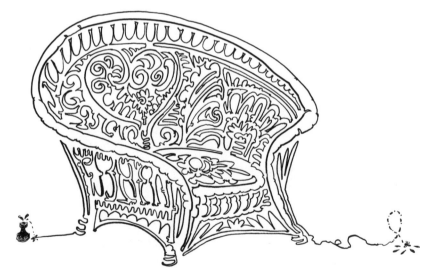

The One Marvelous Thing

The night before Ellen went shopping with Pat, she dreamed she was gazing at a painting that created the illusion of a portal opening upon a grove of citrus trees. Within it a naked goddess tossed grain to a large rose-colored bird. Awakening alone in a room so banal it made her weep, she dressed for the day without enthusiasm.

Ellen has never liked Pat. A child of inherited wealth, Pat is addicted to the buying and selling of properties. The neighborhood is rife with seedy real estate made over into Tuscan villas. Everywhere you look, unedifying brass kokopellis tirelessly tootle on a glut of green. Weird Vietnam vets and old folks too stunned to answer a doorbell have been swapped for earnest acrobats of both sexes. They canter past at all hours accompanied by dogs the size of Hondas sporting alpaca leg warmers. Sundays their gimlet-eyed brats shriek from atop toy castles constructed of Indonesian teak.

Because she dislikes Pat, it makes little or no sense that Ellen accepts to join her shopping. Against her better instincts and before she can change her mind, she is belted into Pat's SUV and already alienated. Today Pat's glazed lips are unfamiliarly swollen, her hair thrashing with extensions, and her contacts tiger agate.

"Enhancement," Pat confides huskily in response to Ellen's eyeballing, "is the name of the game." Ellen, who thinks she is referring to a T.V. program, wonders: "What's it like?"

"Great!" says Pat. "Why settle for less than better?"

"I'm so out of it!" Ellen acknowledges with a small, self-depreciating laugh. "I thought best was good enough."

"Don't be a fool!" Pat scolds her. "Best can *always* be bested! Lamb chops, pesto, Super Tuscans, sex—" She laughs with all her teeth. "Yes, sex *can* be better! Look in the box. In the back seat."

With difficulty, Ellen twists around, and reaching, feels something notched and carved. A bone whistle? A slip of oiled wood? Claws are they? Teeth! She recoils with horror.

"Uzbekie sex toys!" Pat carols, careening into *Wormwood's* vast parking lot.

•

There is a line, maybe three hundred people, waiting for *Wormwood* to open. Her bosom enhanced with Ralph Lauren counterfeit squash blossoms, Pat marches past them, Ellen in tow and already breathless. Knocking on the great glass doors, Pat manages to get someone's attention.

"We're here!" she shouts gaily, "with All International. You must let us in!" Scowling, a salesclerk shakes his head *no*, but Pat, her steel tempered with honey, insists. "We have an appointment with the manager," she gyrates, "and we're already a little late! Please?" she wheedles, "please? Please?" When the door opens, she gives his hand a squeeze. A moment later they are wading in a sea of leather sofas, all indigo blue.

"Truth *is* the consequences," Pat dogmatizes, "especially of lies. We are *here*," she insists, impatient with Ellen's troubled look, "right where we should be. On top of the food chain."

"Here with All International," Ellen snorts as Pat surges on.

"Stop it, Ellen," Pat says. "Stop being a nincompoop. In a minute the doors will open and those bitches out there will tear the place apart. If we're not on our toes, El, we'll miss out on the one marvelous thing." They are surrounded by recliners, and because Ellen continues to look unconvinced, Pat assures her: "There is *always* one marvelous thing."

A low roar swells and overtakes them. All at once *Wormwood* is thick and fast with women, some piloting anxious looking infants on wheels.

"Shit." Pat snarls. They are making their way around archipelagos of Welsh coffee tables. "Fuck them," she says. "Fuck THAT!" And she bolts.

"What *is* it?" Ellen calls after her. "What's wrong?" Pat has taken off in a dead heat towards a faux antique Roman birdcage over six feet high. Butter yellow and well greased with gold leaf, it glitters. Beside it, a clerk with a nervous disorder fumbles with a credit card.

"You can't have that!" Pat shouts at a startled brunette, handsome and dappled with freckles; "Sorry! But the cage is ours. Take a look," she tells the clerk, "it has a 'hold' ticket on it." Swimming in his red jacket, the geriatric clerk appears dazed.

"There was," the brunette speaks evenly, "no hold on this." Ellen thinks she is lovely, with an open, ironical face.

"Yes there was," Pat lies breezily. "I put a hold on it last night. For All International."

"You can take your All International," the woman says kindly, "and shove it. You and your wimpy sidekick."

Mortified, Ellen cringes. She likes the other woman. Likes her bangs, her hazel eyes, her freckles and her spunk. *I am a wimp* she thinks. *Or I wouldn't be here. Tagging along with Pat!* She looks into the woman's face and smiles.

"What's All International anyway?" the woman asks her, almost tenderly. "I doubt it's real!" Leaning close to Ellen she whispers: "I don't think your friend is, either."

"She isn't," Ellen returns her whisper.

"Give her back her credit card," Pat directs the old codger. "Do it."

"I'm Magda," the woman tells Ellen, and thrillingly touches her wrist there where the pulse quickens.

"I'm waiting!" Pat says, beginning to look scary, "for you to give her back her card! Stop clutching it! For god's sake!"

"You are being abused," Magda tells the clerk, "by a mythomaniac. Don't let yourself be pushed around like that. A man your age!"

Ellen thinks the clerk must be eighty, at least. Like so many elderly Americans forced into servitude, he is held together with denture glue and surgical bolts. He has recently recovered from a hip replacement he could not afford. He cannot recall who saw the cage first; he can barely remember his own name.

"Hugo," Pat says reading his breast pocket, "you remember me. I came in last night before closing and told you to put a hold on the bird cage. You remember me. Hugo."

Hugo considers this. Hugo is, after all, his name. Yet he is frightened. His hands are shaking.

"Don't let her persecute you," Ellen says.

"Fuck you!" Pat shouts. "Fuck you, Ellen! Fucking traitor!"

"I have *birds*, Hugo," Magda tells him. "Thirty Australian Zebra finches. Each one has a name. And when one begins to sing, all the others join in. Zebra finches sing in syncopation. They've been doing so for tens of thousands of years. My birds will find their happiness in this cage—but only if you say so, Hugo. It's up to you." The clerk studies the bird cage with real intensity. "This woman—she'll make a phone booth out of it, a urinal—who knows what? Please, Hugo. Be kind. Process my card."

"Screw her, Hugo!" Pat explodes, "the sentimental twat! Screw her, goddamnit!"

"Hey!" says Hugo.

Pat presses her card upon him, but he pulls himself together, straightening his jacket and balancing on his elevator shoes.

"Now, now . . ." he offers. An ancient fire is stirring in Hugo's hollow chest. In his distant youth he was a missionary, and once convinced a head hunter to embrace the greater Power. He begins to process Magda's card.

"Hugo," says Pat. "What the fuck?"

"I'm a Mormon." Hugo says this with dignity.

"What?" Pat barks, now totally out of control, "what the fuck does that have to do with this transaction? I'll tell you what it has to do with this transaction! Not a fucking thing!"

"I'm a Mormon," Hugo repeats, his teeth all arattle, "and I am offended by your manner, Ma'am. My name is Hugo," he tells Magda who nods and signs the receipt.

"Shit," says Pat. "Fuck this." Stomping off she leaves a stench of sulphur and White Diamonds in her wake. "Fuck you Ellen!" she shouts as she eclipses, "I'll *never* take you shopping again."

•

Later that evening as they lie together sweetly entwined, Ellen asks Magda where her birds are.

"What birds, Pussycat?" Magda yawns, and languorous, stretches.

"The finches," Ellen says. "The thirty synchronized finches."

"I have no finches," Magda tells her.

"What's the cage for, then?" Ellen laughs, heartily amused.

"For you, little one," Magda says, taking Ellen's lower lip between her teeth gently. "To curl up in at your leisure like a cat. Like a cat that has eaten up all the little birds one by one. Their feathers, their feet, their tiny skulls."

"Yes!" Ellen purrs her approval. "And each and every one of those birds is named Pat."

A Suicide

for Laura

Her husband was horrible! He made her so miserable! Despite her restlessness, and the persistence of her muted complaints, he insisted on engaging in fellation in the street, although they lived in rural Alabama and this imperiled them both. Doubtless such persuasions indicated a powerful death wish on his part. And, living with him as she did, she could not help but feel suicidal too, which explains why she went along with his urgings, although she really did not want *to engage in sexual activity in the public road.* (These terms are hers.)

Here are the things about her that turned him on: her somewhat dated manner of speaking (engaging in fellation! The public road!) and dressing (all her clothes looked like they were cut from boiled and beaten wool felt).

Finally one morning she stood at the mirror and took stock of herself. Big breasted with mousy hair, she looked more like a grade school principal than the comic book artist she actually was. She decided to go out and *make herself over.* Within hours she was unrecognizable, even to herself. She had everything spiked—her hair, her shoes, her Perrier, her temper. Disguised, she was transformed. So! It was that easy! And at the end of the day she didn't go home. The marriage was over! Just like that! She never looked back! In fact, she forgot about him in no time at all! His goadings, his skinny neck and reckless requests—everything!

She would never know how he'd die—bludgeoned to death in downtown Birmingham by a redneck preacher wielding a chair. When that happened, she was a hip redhead sporting a diamond stud in a front tooth and living in another state, another city. Her manner of speaking was different, too. For example, she'd say things like: *How cool is that?*

Divorce

There are many reasons why I offer myself—in a manner of speaking—to a staggering number of young men, all Japanese. The divorce above all; the divorce that has so thoroughly exhausted me and what's worse, marked me with a chronic look of irritation so like Mother's.

Naked beneath someone else's sheets, fogged in sorrow's exhalations, I lie in silence, having made a vow despite my compulsion—Trixie would say my weakness—to demonstrate to those in my service that I am a democrat, a good sport—who never farts higher than her ass. I can, when I choose, banter with hair dressers, beauticians, waiters and so forth, with genial wit and what is sometimes erroneously perceived as compassion. But not today. I am not here to entertain. I am here so that they shall wipe that nasty look off my face.

Mother and I are not "two peas in a pod"—although Rolph insists that this is so. I blame my current decrescendo on his mistake. And trust that the new Mrs. Rolph—whose current face is as bare of irritation as a new sink—will, like me, land up under a sheet sooner or later. (In this way a spa is very like the morgue.)

The spa's regimen features roots, pernicious thimblefuls of raw clam juice and a bitter tea. Purged of one's terrible secrets, one is tossed into a miserable hut and thrashed. According to the celebrated doctor who rules this roost, a thrashing is just what the female deserves. And *needs*—if she is to be stricken of the mother's hostility, the father's ineptitude. To be released from the family's burden of inevitable crimes. And there are felted rooms where one may give vent to jealous rage by slapping or stomping on a life-sized doll of wax, a beautiful doll—more beautiful, in fact, than our most hated rivals. Here one may commit lamentable acts either in privacy or among strangers, each one more repulsive than the next: hatchet faced, spindle shanked, squabbish, sore as crabs, starved—some howling or bellowing at the doll, others kicking it in the groin, this one rolling on the floor and humiliating herself at the doll's feet, that one totally unhinged, jumping down its throat and snapping off its head.

I understand the Doctor's rigorous bitterness. Like Daddy, he, too, suffered a ruinous divorce. It is the spa's success that has put him back on his feet. The book tours, the lecture series on PBS, the antioxidants marketed in pretty blue glass bottles. Unlike Daddy and despite the requisite bloodletting, the good doctor *is still thrashing*. He has remarried and the witty luxuries provided here are the indication of his ambivalence. After the thrashings, the rantings, the virtual murders, one is invited to soak in a tub brimming with warm cherry pie filling.

•

Mother has met the good doctor numerous times. Years ago, before she began to seriously grind her teeth and to sag irretrievably, the tabloids hinted at a romance. If pressed, Trixie will gleefully enumerate the Doctor's many faults. She claims he is covered with hair—the sorry outcome of misguided self-medication. *This*, she says, *is why he wears gloves, both inside and out, no matter the weather.* But I have caught sight of him floating past in his white smocks and waffle-soled sneakers, and find his features agreeable. Like Rolph's in the months leading up to the marriage, the Doctor's expression is hopeful. This touches me, for despite my upbringing, I have never fully embraced Trixie's fine skepticism, a brutal skepticism honed on Daddy's irrelevance. (But for cash, Daddy's place in our world was always obscure.) Yet, as a girl, when I saw Trixie's face frozen in the custard of censoriousness, I cringed. However, having learned from Daddy's repeated breaches of propriety that a husband is not to be taken seriously, I began to, and under Trixie's guidance, give Rolph "the works." *Nothing* I told him, *comes for free. A successful marriage*, I was always eager to explain, *is run like a successful business: the wife takes in more than she gives out.* Buoyant with certitude, I was ill-prepared when he eclipsed with the other woman to a place difficult to reach—New Zealand! A lawless place given over to eccentricities I was brought up to mightily distrust.

But, back to Mother. It must be said that Trixie suffers a curious contradiction of character. She is a moralist who uncovers the shameful wherever she pokes her abridged nose and, at the same time, she is a materialist who insists that anything human—anger above all—is *natural*. Her own mightily disagreeable nature for example, her uninhibited complaints and vicious teasing, are all spontaneous, clever and good. Yet the tempers of others leave them open to character assassination. In this way my mother demonstrates a callous disregard for the right of others to practice what she has, in the dark recesses of her heart, perfected.

I do not follow in Trixie's footsteps, not exactly, still . . . Our marriage, Rolph's and mine, was, as Trixie hastens to remind me, run on my terms. Of this I should be proud. As is the divorce. Of this I should be pleased. In the words of my lawyer, *the divorced husband is but broken meat and chaff.* My bitterness is therefore unreasonable, as is the nagging fear—even as I soak in a tub of pie filling—that I have fucked up. And yet . . . here's the thing: should Rolph appear before me this instant in his dapper straw boater and yellow suit saying, "Dammit, Tootsie! Let's pick up where we left off!" I would be unable to articulate the word *yes*. I would be unable to smile. *This* is the problem in a nutshell. Although I have spent many hours before the mirror willing my face back into vitality, it remains hideously entangled.

Strange to tell it, I was once—and not very long ago, either—lovely to see. Youth accounted for it, and the fact that I embodied a moment. I looked remarkable in chinchilla shrugs and artfully shredded suede. I glowed in the sugary haze of an elusive ideal. Even my perpetual irritation, so like Mother's, was considered stylish. And my murderous laughter, a razor rending the air—it, too, was very much appreciated.

Panna Cotta

He is cooking for Lucinda and their friends; their laughter rises and falls above the sound of good Danish butter sizzling in the pan. He serves the trout with toasted almonds and a julienne of caramelized citrus. Ablaze in the candlelight, the dish might be of hammered gold. The moment he sets it down, his friends burst into applause.

"Don't," Lucinda admonishes, or pretends to. "Flattery goes to his head." Will he ever grow accustomed to her teasing? "Fat Head!" From across the table she blows him a kiss. Everyone laughs when he offers up a toast to his "dulcet-tongued Lucinda."

•

He had left his first wife when he realized that she would always be chronically enigmatic. Lucinda isn't enigmatic, she's impalpable. A gadfly, she flits from this to that. As slender-waisted as a child, her elbows and knees are as small and round as ping-pong balls. And she is flagrantly blonde, her skin and hair the color of cream.

Lucinda is a healer. Like a pale hummingbird suspended in the ether, she hovers over her clients who, adrift on grass mats, listen to the soothing ping of wind chimes and hushed platitudes. They learn to trust their intuitions, to discover the healing power of their hands, to share Lucinda's gift, her heightened capacity to know and to name unfathomed humiliations. Summers she teaches female masturbation at the Omega Institute, and this fact never ceases to astonish and inspire them. Week after week they return so that they can live in the world without succumbing to despair. Sometimes their faith in her terrifies him.

If Lucinda is a healer and a telepath, he is not. Granted, he is a good cook, perhaps a great one, but, as she eagerly points out, he does not *get people*. A master in the kitchen, he will always be a babe in the woods when it comes to understanding others. He tells her that one cannot cook without understanding others! Bah! says Lucinda. Of course one can! Well then, why won't she teach him? But no. She is unwilling. Because of the nature of their relationship. Its intimacy.

He wonders: what *is* the nature of their intimacy? And *is* it intimacy, exactly? If it is, why is he so lonely? Then again, it is likely that loneliness is part and parcel of the human condition. Hadn't Lucinda told him that when she carols to her class:

You are lonely!

they gasp and grunt in agreement, and always someone weeps.

Yet his own loneliness dissolves as soon as he enters the kitchen. When he approaches his raw materials, an irresistible music claims him and his staff. The work proceeds seamlessly in a state of grace. When he sets a pan of quail on fire, he embodies the spirit of transformation—something of a monster, eccentric, extravagant, irresistible, incapable of error. Dishes surge forth into the night like stars. Meanness and banality are banished from the dining room. His diners are joyous, celebratory, smarter, kinder. Perfect strangers toast one another suggesting what it is they must try: "The tagine! The hen with apricots! The saffroned risotto! The brandied pears!"

This explosive euphoria gives way to a sagacious quietude. An hour into their meal and his diners grow thoughtful. Like those lucky children who have not yet been smacked, they believe in the goodness of things. His is the sort of food that in a better age would have inspired chamber music.

And Lucinda, too, is swept up and away by what can only be called an intoxication. Her cream in repose, she eats his risotto and takes on a gravitas he finds reassuring. This is how they meet: she at one of his tables silenced and deepened by his risotto.

But this cannot last. One day Lucinda rebels. An esteemed motivator, she cannot stomach to be held in thrall by another for long. Without warning she tells him his cooking reeks of death, his kitchen is a morgue in which cadavers by the dozens are stacked—"Cadavers?" he gasps. "My fresh racks of Oregon lamb?"

His kitchen is a charnel house. Fire, alcohol, spices—all this is not *natural*. His kitchen stinks of war. "Of *war*?" He cannot believe his ears. His feasts are funerals! She will deign to eat his salads, but only if his beets are raw.

"And if I bake you a pie of peacock hearts, my beloved . . . even that would not tempt your sharp tongue? Will you, my dearest, never again *eat me*?"

"Horrible!" she calls him. "Horrible man! *Mortician!*" she sputters and seethes. "How dare you tease me! How dare you question my personal life choices?"

He proposes an encyclopedic platter of cheese. She professes a horror of *grease*—she who had so recently loved his bechamels and brown butters. *She fears death*, he supposes. *The body's corruption.* When on those rare occasions she enters the restaurant to graze on celery and salt, she glowers at the other diners with visible repugnance. *Virtual cadavers eating cadavers!*

He begins to dislike her.

•

In her company, he is now hang-dogged. Poor soul! He begins to entertain something like paranoia. And this because he can no longer share with his beloved a passion for pig trotters, braised rabbit and soft-shelled crabs. Instead he must listen to her endless chatter about her own career; she speaks of it and of her clients with a certain fevered animation. Her clients desire her; well of course they do. Doesn't she stoke their fires? Dizzy with fear he asks if she returns their heat.

"Well," she replies, with a new haughtiness, "one can't rebuff what one has inspired. Not when healing is involved."

"Ah. Yes. But . . . ," he insists. "Surely. Having been, ah. Warmed by your, uh. *Ministrations*. (He hates the word, archaic and clumsy—yet finds no other.) Couldn't they, can't they, I mean. Well. You've liberated them after all to go elsewhere, to live, passionately *elsewhere*. Are you. Must you. Must you be *all* things to them? The medium," he strokes her cheek, "and the prize?" (How he struggles for his words!)

He has broken into a sweat and his hands are perceptibly shaking. Seeing how distraught all this has made him, she reaches into his shirt and caresses a nipple.

"I only let them hold me, and only sometimes. Just a hug, darling. As is acceptable among friends. And then I send them on their way, reassured! Empowered! So that yes—that's it, exactly! Off they go to get *it on*! With somebody else." She sings these last three words in a voice he recognizes as Madonna's. "I'm a facilitator! Not a dominatrix!"

If this is true, why is it that whenever he is in the house alone, he finds himself stalking the clothes in her closet for clues? He stares at her silk saris, the Indonesian scarves and gilded sandals and cannot help but imagine her embracing a client on the floor after hours like a Tantric temple whore providing at once something sacred and profane. He pokes through scraps of paper in her desk drawers and although he feels a fool still his heart pounds because of the terrible danger he is in—desiring, disliking and distrusting a woman simultaneously. Instead of attending to the myriad things his life demands, he finds himself dialing a phone number scribbled on the back of a small square paper napkin.

Drained of blood, he listens to a message in an unfamiliar male voice that seems smug, somehow, and also suggestive. Putting down the receiver he finds himself thinking: *Well. All people are impossible. It just depends on how long one knows them and how much one can bear.* He considers the possibility that what he has always thought of as her openness, her boundless enthusiasm, is all due to a lack of self awareness and an unusually thick skin. And if she is a narcissist? Enamored of her own powers to liberate and enslave? That night as she sleeps, he dials the number on the napkin. This time the man answers. "Peggy?" he says. "Peg?" Aw! Sweetheart! Don't hang up!"

Sometimes, she tells him, she waives her fees. Doesn't that imply the relationship has tumbled into lubricity? Considering what he fears—fears! It keeps him up nights!—the waivered fee is the proof of his cuckoldry—an outdated word, a foolish word—but one that satisfies his mood. When he attempts to discuss this, she loses her temper and tells him with real anger that he has no business at all, none whatsoever, prying into her professional life.

"Do I ask you?" she shouts, "what goes on in the kitchen? How do I know you're not buggering your cheflings in the larder?"

He becomes unraveled. His mind wanders. He pierces this thumb with a fish knife. He is a powerfully built man who suffers a helpless sensation in his knees. Briefly he considers suicide, a dramatic seppuku in the middle of his kitchen on a busy Saturday night. If only he knew how to, he would break down and sob. Their impending breakup is now common knowledge.

When he walks into his own glass-fronted door and chips a tooth, he knows he must pull himself together.

Exhausted at ten in the morning, he throws himself on his office floor and falls asleep. He dreams of a fantastic panna cotta—a savory panna cotta of outstanding flavor and size. His dream is a revelation, and his sleep refreshing.

He invites their friends to a feast to celebrate the inevitable separation. He throws himself into an event that will transform his longing and his rage into something like beatitude; a profound satisfaction, sweetly vertiginous. He cooks his way out of the end of the affair, and feeling joyous puts on a tuxedo.

When everyone arrives the table is rife with candles. In the center, a panna cotta Lucinda crouches sphinxed, cuffed and socked in sashimis and lobster queuelles. If the panna cotta is one-third life size, still it is wonderfully impressive, the way a suckling pig or entire roasted lamb is impressive. The panna cotta is served on a platter of old faience—a thing a museum curator would die for.

•

Lucinda is seated at the head of the table, and at once suffers a stunning realization. Her months of extreme asceticism are founded in guilt; she has, after all, been sleeping with a client. She acknowledges the toast in her honor: from her end of the table, she gazes at him with renewed affection.

"I feel," she says, "like the lead in a film by what's his name." She accepts a plate of sashimi, cannot resist the quenelles, nor the panna cotta, studded as it is, with bronzed scallops.

His imagination is unleashed; he feels happier than he has in months, and dashing. With unaccustomed ferocity of humor, he tells a story of one Metrocles, a student of Aristotelian philosophy, who having devoured a deep dish of spiced lima beans, farts publically in the midst of an oration. Profoundly ashamed, Metrocles tumbles into a melancholy so extreme he can no longer sleep or eat. As he approaches death, his friends convince him to return to class one last time. There his teacher, Crates, farts so eloquently in his pupil's favor, his life is saved. Metrocles goes on to become a philosopher of consequence—and a gourmet of delicate tastes.

His friends' laughter unleashes him further. He proposes that a stomach is like a brain; it has a mind of its own, it suffers fevers, tantrums, sleepless nights, fits of longing and self loathing. In other words, the stomach "has a soul!" He says something strange:

"The stomach is an intermittent sarcophagus." But before anyone can ask him what that means, he leaps ahead: "I mean a *factory*! Turning raw materials into bricks more or less cooked!"

"Speaking of *cooked*!" Lucinda calls out from her end of the table, "grill me a cutlet, sweetheart, or two? A rack! Of that organic Oregon Lamb!"

But no. He tells her: tonight the menu is *fixe*. *She* is all there is to eat. However, he agrees with her; she makes for a fine hors d'oeuvre, but not for a satisfactory meal. At this remark the handsome wife of a mutual friend, an aspiring vintner, abroad, laughs aloud. With a pang of real unhappiness, Lucinda knows she has just been eclipsed. And he? He continues to suggest the oddest things. He says:

"The moment one swallows a live oyster, one might as well be a boa constrictor."

"A boa constrictor," Lucinda's sudden rival breathes, "or a wolf in a fairy tale. Swallowing lambs and babes entire!" The rival is radiant, brown as toast spread over with honey. "Your riddle," she continues, "the one that goes: "Why is a stomach like an intermittent sarcophagus? I know the answer."

"Why?" he asks, gazing at her with intensifying interest.

"Because it is only the first step on a protracted rite of passage."

The table explodes with laughter. Everybody laughs except Lucinda that is, whose cream has begun to visibly turn. And to recede.

A Secret Life

for R.C.

retel's father was Viennese, as was his father, and his father's father before him. They looked alike, and Gretel took after them. Gretel's favorite pastime was to ponder their portraits in the family album. She appreciated the fact that they all lived well into their nineties, and were—as was Gretel—shaped like pears. When among her peers she lagged behind on her bike, or proved unable to scale a tree, Gretel recalled the sturdy paternal line and was assured that, if her life was unexceptional, it would last a long time. For this reason her appetite was good, even exemplary. She appreciated the *wurstels* and *schlagobers* her mother, an American, had taken pains to master. She slept without dreaming, was well behaved, punctual, without ambition, tidy. She liked doing things for her papa, such as fetching his rolled paper from the front stoop and, on wash days, folding his socks. When he trimmed his moustache, she watched and saw to it that no hair fell on the soap.

Her father had come to America as a boy, but had never left Vienna in his mind. He extolled her qualities whenever he could: the café counters piled high with cake, the many preparations for cabbage, the incessant, merry ringing of tram bells. He told of how he had often been beaten with bundles of switches, and that an infamous Viennese Jew named Freud had been born with a mane of coal black hair.

•

Gretel liked it when her father told her she was a *model Viennese*; she liked it when he chucked her playfully beneath her rounded chin, or pinched a dimpled cheek. A *model Viennese*, she did her papa's bidding gladly. Should she disgrace herself, she'd turn her back to him, lift her skirt and without a whimper, wait for the smack. When over the evening bratwurst it was announced that they would be setting off for Vienna as soon as school was out, Gretel became so pink her mother feared a fever and gave her a tall glass of iced licorice water to sip slowly. A few days later her father presented her with a pocket diary in which to inscribe her thoughts each day. Because the pages were illustrated with things Viennese—a *dudelsack* (or Austrian bag pipe), the Austro-American Institute, the university chemical laboratory—there was room for only a very brief thought.

That night, buttoned up in her flannel pyjamas, and this despite the mildness of the weather, Gretel took up a stub of pencil and wrote, with letters so round and pale they might have been inscribed in bubblebath:

WE SHALL GO TO VIENNA WHERE
PAPA WAS BORN AND WHERE HIS
PAPA WAS BORN. TONIGHT WE
ATE BRATWURST.

•

From the first instant, Vienna delighted Gretel. She took to the equestrian statuary, the bronze river gods spouting water, the beer gardens where her father surprised her by drinking a great deal of beer. Their hotel, der Dudelsack, on the corner of Angst-neurosestrasse and der Minderwertiggasse provided liberal boxes of ham sandwiches and salami, and these they trotted about on their daily excursions. Gretel saw with satisfaction that the Viennese ladies whom her father acknowledged with approving glances were all plump. She admired der Dudelsack's restaurant, its beams as black as her father's tortoiseshell glasses, and above all, its napkins that lay weightily on one's lap and knees. The napkins were rolled and folded into irresistible shapes: crowns and roses, dunce caps and boats, palm trees and flutes.

They ate

NOODLES WITH MELTED BUTTER
AND NUTMEG. BREADED VEAL.

They ate plenty of breaded veal in Vienna, and pastries bloated with *schlagobers*. They ate pigs' knuckles and at the opera cracked their hard boiled eggs on the chair backs of the persons in front of them. Her mother assured her that the shells would be swept up later; indeed, she had seen a young girl in an apron standing in the shadows with her broom. In the meantime, Gretel could enjoy The Magic Flute, smartly crack her egg and hold it, clean and cool, in her palm against her cheek, before taking a nice big bite.

After the opera, they each had a slice of layer cake, spread with raspberry jam and glazed with bittersweet chocolate. Noodles, breaded veal, boiled eggs, chocolate cake—it was altogether too much. Until very late, Gretel was agitated.

•

Although Vienna is in the throes of an early summer, Gretel is up to her neck in flannels and a feather comforter. Beneath her foams a feather bed. An hour passes, then another. She is thinking of der Dudelsack's lovely linen tablecloths and those allusive napkins—so artfully pleated and tucked, with creases so deep that when she dips her fingers into them, they vanish. And she wonders: who spends her days in the pantry folding napkins? Who trained her? Is there an academy in Vienna where girls are taught the art of napkin folding? And now:

Gretel imagines them. Row after row of model Viennese girls in their pinafores at their little desks, each one with her iron in hand and a snowy napkin. They have been at it so long the tips of their fingers, the knobs of their knuckles are sore, and their bottoms, too. And should a girl cause an unintentional crease, she is scolded by the Mistress of Napkin Folding Herself, told to lift her skirts, and, utterly exposed is smartly smacked.

Sandwiched between her feather bed and comforter, Gretel's world is heating up so fast she thinks she is very like a fat dumpling, round and white and steaming hot. Rolled in sugar, she ignites.

In her fever dream she presses napkins with astounding dexterity—or so she thinks, her little desk piled high. Ah! But no! The Mistress of Napkin Folding, as thin and black as a poker, has seized her by an ear. Within the instant, Gretel is tossed over her bony knee and smacked.

"I told you to make the 'Javanese Temple!'" The Mistress of Napkin Folding booms as the other girls titter (although some, recalling past humiliations are quietly weeping). "Not the 'Pig in the Poke!' Take this! And that! And this! And that! From this day on, naughty Gretel, you will never forget The Mistress of Napkin Folding!"

•

Morning comes. Gretel is roused by her papa who must violently shake her. "The flannels," he scolds her mother, "are far too hot for summer! See what a state our Gretel is in!" Sentenced to silence for the rest of the morning, her mother bows her head.

Gretel is made to take a cooling bath. Dressed in a crisp Viennese pinafore and apron—an outfit that should she wear it to school in the fall will elicit hoots of laughter—she cautiously descends the waxed stairs that twist and turn downwards into der Dudelsacks's dining room. She breakfasts on cheese and tongue and fruit and sweet rolls and cucumbers—the whole washed down with bowls of chicory. Unlike the ones at dinner, the breakfast napkins are neatly pressed into triangles. Their folds are deep, and Gretel slides her fingers inside and out of them. Is there a waiter? A waitress? In later years she will have no memory of them, but only of her papa waiting for her to finish her breakfast, his hands wedged beneath his buttocks. She hates to see him sitting thus. An odd habit. Sometimes her papa's behavior is incomprehensible. For example, he has bought himself a pipe. He alone smokes it, yet he insists Gretel's mother keep the pipe cleaners and tobacco in her purse.

Gretel's father is eager to visit der Allgemeines Krankenhaus, to see for himself if it is, indeed, the largest hospital on the continent. It is fortunate for both Gretel and her mother that an irritable bureaucrat will not allow them access to the Krankenhaus's forty acres. Off they fly instead to a manufactory of barometers where they are left to journey an immense room in which barometers, thousands of them, are set out on tables as far as the eye can see. Barometers are also suspended from the ceiling and walls. Some look like birdhouses with porches; others like the castles one encounters in fish tanks.

Depending on the inscrutable workings of the weather, either a little lady—dressed as Gretel is dressed—or a little man, will appear all alone on a porch or a castle balcony. Or it is a priest or a devil, Adam or Eve, Saint George or the dragon, Jesus in the cradle or crucified, a plate of sausage or a plate of fish. As her parents are unable to decide, they are directed to a manufactory of cuckoo clocks just down the street where Gretel is at once impressed by a minute circle of Viennese School girls who, at the sound of chimes ringing the hour, slide out from a tiny garden gate and circumvent the clock's face and inner workings—cleverly hidden from view. After a brief discussion, her parents buy a clock of the classic sort, sporting a cuckoo with, or so Gretel thinks, an unforgivably stupid expression on its face.

They have just enough time to return to the barometers before supper, where they purchase a dour little couple condemned to a lifetime of simultaneous isolation and proximity for, Gretel realizes with a shudder, they can never be in the same place at the same time.

Although the rigors of the day have thoroughly exhausted Gretel, still she polishes off her cutlet and before falling asleep, The Mistress of Napkin Folding exacts a full measure of punishment.

•

The next day Gretel and her parents visit a nearby castle in which are displayed salt cellars dating from the eighteenth century. One of these takes its inspiration from the sea; its three fused cups sit on a bed of coral, and the shell at its crown serves as a handle. The arrangement evokes a particularly fanciful folded napkin; its shells and cups clamor to be touched. When next day they come upon rows of fingerbowls, Gretel nearly swoons.

"Hand washing," her mother speaks with evident nostalgia and for the first time that day, "was once a sort of ceremony."

The impact of the word 'ceremony' on Gretel's imagination is phenomenal; it quickens her.

"Only the fingertips," her mother murmurs, lost in a dream of her own, "should touch the water."

An extensive collection of snuff boxes, some made to look like figs with hinges, precipitate a new set of private associations. Gretel's precocious interest in antiquities causes her parents to nod at one another with satisfaction.

Before leaving the castle they climb its tower to admire the view of the Danube and surrounding hills and plains from the Alps to the Carpathians. As her papa sputters with nostalgia the world shivers in its haze beneath them. In later years Gretel will recall the immense silence of the moment although, in fact, birds are rioting in the trees, and on the tower stairs, tourists, and in her father's pockets, coins. The afternoon ends at a haberdasher's where, as Gretel furtively fingers a pleated dickey, her father buys himself a hat ornamented with a miniature whisk.

That evening, bathed in the eternal twilight of der Dudel-sack's opaline ceiling lamps, Gretel does not notice her father's voice rolling around the room like a great suet pudding. She does not notice the voices of the other diners, nor the music that is being played at the far end of the room. She does not covet the eidelweiss stuck in its little flute of glass. Yet a disapproving glance suffices to keep her from toying with her napkin and, again, from prodding her delicately folded sweetbread turnover with the little golden spoon intended for the after-dinner demitasse. And when the dessert omelet overtakes the table as though a cumulus cloud had chosen to squat there, she gasps with surprise.

•

The academy is now the size of a castle. Blazing like ice beneath the moon, it sits smack on a black needle of stone. A place of blizzards, high winds, tumultuous weather. Impossible to reach; impossible to escape. A castle, yes, sitting high in the sky and yet the sun never seems to reach it. Below, far below in the summer meadows the sun shines, but not here. An ancient place, its clocks are hexed. Time moves back and forth in two directions, only. *Dawn*! the cuckoo cries once and then, within the instant: *Dusk*!

The castle is grand, yet has no central heating, no elevator or baths. Only spare faucets of scalding water for which the girls scramble in the dark before being confronted by a breakfast that they are forbidden to touch. Indeed, the castle is mined with explosive temptations that, despite the dangers, are impossible to resist. Hungry and improperly washed, the girls stand in their thin pinafores and buttoned boots to weather the day's instructions.

The castle's interior unfolds onto marble halls and deep stairwells. There are sooty kitchens where maidens in spotless aprons are threatened with undisclosed vicissitudes. Here: a door opens to reveal a perpetual theater where instructive tableaux are staged. There: chastened maidens sweep between spankings. Across the hall, the library's heavy ledgers record each infraction in thick, black ink. And on every floor are rooms where lessons are taught: the correct use of starch. Pipe cleaners. Spoons. (It does not occur to Gretel to consider the castle cellars, its dungeons and crypts. For now the upper castle, alone, suffices.)

It is rumored that beyond the moat and thickets a park lies hidden. An obelisk and a grotto are cradled in the hedges. Should Gretel manage to escape the castle and reach the park, she will discover a small garden gate overgrown with briars. A gentle push, the briars fall away, and she is released from the castle's inexorable cogs and gears. Gretel descends a nearly perpendicular path and, looking down, sees the twinkling lights of the city.

•

That night when Gretel's papa steals a look at his daughter's diary, he is perplexed by an emblematic yet somehow expressive series of associations:

BEE ROSE IRIS LILY FLUTE CRAB
PALMTREE TAPER BOAT JAVENESE
TEMPLE OBELISK GROTTO

—and a line (does he recognize Horace?) taken from a clock or a barometer, perhaps, or possibly, a snuff box:

Here find a hid recess where
Life's revolving day
In sweet delusion softly
Steals away . . .

The Ominous Philologist

The doubled pearl is likened to twins who, by birth interlarded, rattle one another's tempers. The doubled pearl, *phlap-phlap*, personifies that human rarity, as does the double-flapped felt hat. Tradition dictates a visor: *laptop*—likewise the indication of anything that has a preceding part or protrusion, that prods the future or the backside of the bride.

—The anomalous deserves our attention.

The groom, *tiplap*, another felt hat word, indicates a Tartar root: to press, to prick, to fricate; to cook beneath a cover, to compress; hairy, itchy, prickly; a thing that causes a rash. *Tiplap* is also the word for woolen goods that come in twos: felt slippers, the ears of Tartar sheep, and, by extension, rugs made of hair.

A coarse woolen overcoat, *topcoat*, is the demonstration of the root's evolution. In Spain, *topcoat* is a "thing of little value." *Topcoat* suggests felt of poor quality. Indeed, it should come as no surprise that in these regions, anything *phlap-phlap* and *topcoat* are said to "dissolve in fog." (Note that in Portuguese the initial attricata, *pf*, has advanced to simple *f*, while the medial and final *pp* has retrograded to *p*: *flapflap*.)

—The infidel will stew his pearls in pork.

Two kinds of pearls are of interest here: those doubled: *phlap-phlap*, and those twinned: *icepop*. Twinned they are separate entities, *pop-pop*; doubled, a pearl is merely conjoined.

Again, *laptop* designates a state of being or a thing that is "always ahead of itself." The same could be said of my colleagues who do not bother to read me but press recklessly, *turnpike*, in the fog of contention, ill dressed for the inclement weather of dispute. The jampan driver who longs for the rump that flashes in the greener grass of virtuality is *laptop*. Like circus freaks, fornicators are rolled into one (tosspot).

—The infidel will drop his pants and squat in full view of steeples: *potluck*.

Although my rival, Uma Harishchandra, has strenuously battled my thesis both in public and privately: *trouser*, I continue to insist that the first born of twins is *laptop*, i.e., the one who enters first into the air, the one who, in the state of being previous, is also known as the beak, the nose, the snout, the elbow.

Like the nose and knees, the elbow is given priority, *dishtop*, in space and time. Ditto the lump on the head and, by extension, the first thing seen as the fog of unreason lifts.

—Unreason is the bane of the philologist.
—Once the oyster has swallowed its pearl, it grows into a tree.

The felt hat, *tophat*, designates those beads of glass forced upon the mollusk to irritate the nacreous precipitate. A pearl of poor quality is said to be botched; it is a *washpot*, the "face of a woman dead for a week"; a *tossout*. In her clitoral frenzies, the bipolar Harishchandra insists that the botched pearl is *tossup*; she is confusing *tossup* with *two bats*: the empty oyster and, by extension, the blown egg and the broken head. In this way does philology become a crime.

Prior to her murder, *two bats*, as yet unsolved, my colleague had the temerity to propose that in certain seasons, the oyster sails the seas much as bees sail the air. This is clearly ridiculous. Only a madwoman would speak of oysters and bees in the same breath. "They sail in flocks beneath the moon with their shells open." My reader will agree: there is no room for poetry in philology.

—When provoked, a philologist will prove venomous.

Pliny suggests that a thought flitting across the mind of a parent will influence the features of the unborn child. The child will tumble into the world incarnate of an idea. Perhaps the

 doubled pearl suggests the same phenomenon. Mirrored in God's infinite grace, the divine notion of a pearl precipitates a second, but worldly. In this way, everything in the palpable universe is the corporealized double of an idea. The thought of bashing in a rival's skull: *two bats*, *pit stop*, will generate the act.

The Dickmare

It all boils down to this: does she present to the Dickmare or not? She fears the lot of them, those perpetually inflated Dickmares, their uncanny magnetism matched only by their startling lack of symmetry. Yet she has been summoned. A thing as unprecedented as it is provoking.

And she has awakened with a curious rash. It circles her body like a cummerbund. A rash as florid as those coral gardens so appreciated by lovers of bijouterie. A rash having surged directly—or so she supposes—from her husband's anomalous—or so she hopes—behavior.

Once she had thought her husband admirable. Admirable his thorny cone, his sweet horny operculum, his prowess as a swimmer, the beauty of his sudden ejections, the ease with which he righted himself when overturned. Not one to retreat into his shell, in those days his high spirits percolated throughout the yellow mud they optimistically called home.

Adolescents intellectually annihilated by lust and hopeful mysticisms would engage her husband for hours on end with thorny topics such as why Noah built the Ark without once questioning the High Clam's outburst of temper. And if the High Clam loves the fishes and the shelled fishes best (after all they did not suffer during the forty days and nights of rain but, instead, benefited)—why were they snatched in numbers from their naps and served up Top Side boiled in beer and dressed with hot butter? And her husband instructed the small fry with cautionary tales featuring the terrible Kracken who swims on the surface of the waves like a gigantic swan downing mischievous little mollusks at will—the fear of the lie quieting both their wanderlust and their exuberance (and some were so shellacked with fear they slammed shut never to be heard from again).

The old timers, too, came to her husband for advice, sleepless in expectation of those fearsome migrations they were impelled to entertain periodically for reasons beyond everyone's grasp. It seemed that everybody was in need of advice all the time, anymore, and that her husband's ministry never ceased.

At first she had been proud of his popularity, or rather, had done her best not to hate the constant tide of traffic and bavardage. She would shut her eyes and cling to anything, to debris—a rotting hull, a stump of pier, a branch of folifera. And she would dream unfructuous dreams of the secret arms of rivers that are said to feed the sea—uncertain waters flowing from an unknowable source (because Top Side)—a source she wished to find.

•

Her husband's popularity came to a sudden halt right after a doleful interlude with the Cuckfield quintuplets whom he had surprised in their daily rotations over by Sandy Bottoms. Now no one, not even the Squamosas who wear their digestive tubes in their arms—will give either of them the time of day. Once so admired, her husband has taken his problems to a Dickmare—and there is a scary rhyme the small fry trill about him:

When the moon is out
and the bivalves hop—
and cannot stop,
and cannot stop,
and a shadow steals above . . .
tell me! What is it?
What is it? My love!

—a Dickmare who orders up nacreous pills from the oyster shop, pills that resemble toothed hinges and once swallowed, produce an egg capable of sprouting fins and swimming. These days her husband's conversation is as rare as a clam's liver. He has lost the instinct for cordiality, and his capacity for mobility is sorely compromised. He has developed two pairs of bocal palpi, and even if he had wanted to, she would not want him to kiss her. When in motion he takes no great strides, but instead stretches out his foot so slowly that she—who stands at the ready with a glass of water (these days his thirst is prodigious)—fears the tedium will kill her. But then, having set the right foot down, he withdraws the left so suddenly that, crying out, she drops the tumbler, wetting her apron. When he is mercifully out the door, another unexpectedly vigorous push with his left foot sends him headlong into his vehicle.

Is it a squid or a calamar?

•

 When her husband returns he wishes to engage her. Occupying the recliner, he kneels on his knuckles, inching forward with one hand on each end of the apparatus. This, she fears, may lead to further disability. She can tell he has taken the other pills, the ones the size of a grain of linseed, which, like those the size of a split pea, and unlike those the size of a small haricot bean, are, at the instant of ingestion, spat out upon the floor. She stands at the ready, her small broom resting at her side.

The fine salmon pink of her husband's cheeks has darkened, and his skin exudes a peculiarly pungent odor reminiscent of dead eels. Provoked by the prescribed medicaments, within the hour she knows he will turn upon himself like a wheel in motion.

Her husband displays his lamellar and vivid portions. He wishes to excite her curiosity as, he tells her, she has excited the Dickmare's who, having asked to see her photograph and at once been satisfied, extends an invitation to his grotto. The Dickmare suggests that she is distinguished from the schools of others of her kind, by a brilliancy of eye that, added to her moist plumpness, renders her *the most appealing analysand he could aspire to*. She is *a treasure, the single form reflected in a plurality of lesser forms, or, rather, she* is *that plurality reflected in a singular form*.

Unclear as to what he has said, still she cannot help but be moved—as creatures such as she, so fraught with disappointments, swarm within his reach, easy prey for lesser contenders, those who do not have access as the Dickmares do, to the tops of rocks, nor have they access to the medicines. And it is true: she is lovely, vitreous and permeable, her bottom globulous. Aroused, she is luminous in the dark. So round, so smooth, so readily ablaze in her posterior part! No one, she muses, has noticed these things for a very long time. And  so, after all these months watching her husband pull himself across the floor in fractions—a transaction that is always accompanied by frequent vomitings and the prodigious thirst—she weighs her chances. Risky business!

Or is it a Dick . . .

After all, the Dickmares are known to unspool and push their pistons forward with such alacrity, a subconical cavity will be stunned into service before it has a chance to ignite. And she fears that rather than excite his compassion, the curious rash now tumbling to her knees like a Samoan's grass skirt will excite his scorn and what's more his wrath. Yet it is also true that she has just that morning shed her shell—a thing both temporary and wildly appealing. If she is at her most vulnerable, she is also at her most charming. The rash, she hopes, may well be a function of this transformation, her heightened state. Her beauty—she can see it now—has never been more poignant.

It boils down to this: might the Dickmare provide a pill less bitter than the one she has sucked ever since the Cuckfield fry gave voice to their many peculiar complaints? Might the Dickmare assuage her loneliness and her humiliation? Is she afflicted enough to dare seek out a questionable success with an Upper Mudder known to be sensuous, furious and cruel? And she so fragile! So amply furnished with tender sockets and delicate rosettes rotundular and soft. Yes, above all *she is soft*. And so easily impressed!

It is said at Death—and once the flesh has dissolved into the limitless bodies of things so small they cannot be per-

ceived by the naked eye—the soul is swept away by a current called Forgetfulness and carried to an edifice of foam so impalpable no one has ever seen it. She wants to be the one to see it and to inform the others as to its nature.

Blue Funk

People love my city for its brasseries like hothouses, ardent and perverse, its breezes that smell of coffee and of the sea. But when I am in my blue funk I see nothing of all this. Which is why I did not notice the dress shop sooner, although it is on a street familiar to me. For one thing there is the tavern. Its décor recalls my city's imperialist past. One sips rum late in felted spaces. Or dips one's bread in a purple sauce, a sauce my city is famous for, made of shallots and red wine. The tavern has rooms to let, and once when my lover and I had drunk far too much, we took a bed upstairs. Our room was ruled by shadows and rumors of the lovemaking of strangers.

The streets of my city are named for things that have vanished: Mirror Street, Jew Street, The Street of Cakes. Because it rains often, the cobbles appear to be greased. Each afternoon the sky uncoils with a hiss. The darkness of the street enters into the houses, and everywhere you can hear the window shutters slam shut.

When I saw the shop suspended in the blue haze of autumn, I was attracted by its windows of bubbled glass, its spills of silk the color of sour milk. The shop's witch beckoned me, her smile like a gate. She was uncommonly pale and thin, and like a beached fish, had lost her sheen. Yet I was spellbound.

Such is the perverseness of my temperament. I can go for days in limbo, a sleepwalker devoid of desire, and then tumble into therapeutic forms of terror. I allow myself to be mesmerized by the unscrupulous. I have paid strangers to break my fingers. I have attempted to swallow the sea. Determinisms my therapist (who is, in fact, a puzzle even to himself) is unable to fathom.

Inside the shop the witch was steaming the creases from a new shipment of silk dresses with her wand. The air was humid and smelled of silk and the mirrors fogged over. Already I felt better, cleaner—although I'd been on my feet for hours, maybe days, trying to shake off the blue funk. My feet were grey with dust; I had tracked the dust of the city into the shop. I had tracked in my black confusion.

Vitreous things in cases beckoned me and suddenly I wanted to be beautiful again, to everywhere be followed by eyes. I saw a heavy choker of transparent spheres seeded with what looked like black caviar. I wanted it as much as I had wanted my fingers broken, or to be fucked in a dangerous part of town. And there were coral rings burning with tangerine flames, and soft leather gloves as green as new money.

The witch handed me a scarf like smoke weighted down with shards of glass. Although I held it against me with caution, its fabric shredded easily. Torn fabric has always caused my heart to ache, a heavy sphere to rise within my throat. A feeling I would kill for, because when it is not choking me, my blue funk conceals me like a cloak. Outside, the city darkened and stilled and I could hear the rain thrashing on the roof. The witch gave me a dress the color of dusk. It was a marvelous color, like the dreaming iris of an eye, shifting from spangled vermillion to green. I took it from her gratefully, and for a time forgot everything: the city and its misfortunes, the tavern and its shadows, my blue funk, and faded beauty, my eternal loneliness, everything.

The witch's dressing room was very narrow with a high ceiling. Outside the air was panting, and the street, flooding. Already the water roiled at my ankles. And the dress! The dress spilled over my body like water except for the pin that, caught to a seam, pricked me, causing me to shiver with longing. As the water nipped my breasts, a bracelet toothed towards me. When it snapped at my wrist, my hand swam into it.

"Go to the mirrors!" the witch cried from behind her counter, and I did. From mirror to mirror, scaled in the flames of youth, those treacherous flames. The witch's mirrors awakened a forgotten hunger for the world, an imperious, an insatiable, a devastating hunger that I knew could never be shaken.

In the past, contagion and death ravaged my city, assuring silence in the streets. But now affluence assures that when it rains, the streets are empty. People are in the shops, trying on blonde and silver furs. Or they are eating pastries in the many teashops that line the central square, or enjoying a late afternoon movie, or taking an early supper in one of the magnificent boats moored at the water's edge.

Who's There?

I fell asleep thinking that if I could understand the languages of pelicans, I would be delighted by their sense of humor which I imagine is akin to Edward Lear's—a man who so often saw birds in people, and people in birds.

In the middle of the night, someone shouted *Honda* in my ear, and I was aroused from a profound slumber with the terrible knowledge that the anticipated campaign had begun. I wondered what god-damned word they'd hit me with next, and if I would be awakened like this often. Yet, as I warmed my milk on the hot plate, I was reassured because I had no intention whatsoever of buying a Honda—quite the contrary. It seemed to me that the beaming of the name in the middle of my rest was akin to an unwanted finger up my ass. I vowed that I would not buy a Honda, not ever, not even if my life depended on it. Yet, such interruptions: *Pearlmutter! Pie-cake! Giblets!*, should they be frequent, could lead to irresistible rage. I imagined *running amok*, as the tight-assed missionaries used to say about folks whose tranquil lives they had perturbed with filthy fables of saviors born in stables and served up to heaven like shashlik on a stick. Should I *run amok*, I will reveal myself to the Powers as *one who is no shopper*.

As of Thursday, the sidewalks are capable of detecting the absence of credit cards and wallets in a person's pockets, and of reducing that person to slush. The day is dawning when some of us are to be made into wastewater as others are buying Hondas online. There is nothing to do but return to bed and wait for the knock on the door. When it comes I will be aroused from a dream of priests with beaks carrying bats and bricks with which to strike me down.

The Scouring

How grateful I am for The Scouring! The physical world, once so overwhelming, is now reduced to level planes and we may press onward, fearless of obstructions. I recall with a certain residual horror, the fetid smells so common in my youth, the stench of rotting vegetable matter, of blossoms wantoning in the untamed season called "Spring," the aggravation of birdsong, the heady impositions of "Summer" when the birdbaths were green with the scum of stagnant water. Then "Fall"—its rank odors of dead leaves, the terrible bodies of things that scuttled about in those leaves, the persistence of slugs ... One might have, within an hour, been harried by a butterfly or worse: a moth, a wasp, a bee, or a spider stewing in its own malevolence right under one's very bed! (I almost forgot "Winter," that season of damp basements.)

The New Generation has no inkling of these things. They could not care less. I do not wish to burden them with my stories of the past and its baroque intrusions. It would be criminal to trouble their placid velocities, the ordered economy of their meditations with my relic tales of obstacles overcome. They know nothing of The Scouring, the horrors of The Transition, the blind optimism of The Reconstruction. This is how it should be. The New Generation is serene, propelled like beams of light—not yet disembodied, although this will surely come. Together we sweep across the globe in imitation of the cosmical machine. The sound of wind—the wind of our own making—is the only sound we hear. No footfalls, no gnashing of teeth, no conversation. We are no longer the playthings of the weather, gossip, temper or appetite.

For a time, it is true, I missed the smells of cooking, and in the secret sanctum of my kitchen—now off limits—I did not neutralize the air, but instead heightened the experience—now impossible to describe—by sealing the windows and the door. I'd make a stew of lamb, say, or bake a gingerbread—not to eat them, mind you, (for already we had overcome the vicious cycles of corporeal servitude) but to inhale those fragrances. It all seems so very long ago! I would luxuriate (please—not a word of this to anyone!) in the scrubbing of the pots and pans. (In the old days I was considered soft: a man who liked to cook! A stupid activity. Cooking, like sex, stimulates all the senses to an extraordinary degree.)

These days I barely recall the sound of butter sizzling in the pan, but I know it was a thing I much appreciated as a child. And the apples glazed with caramel that shattered against the teeth. (It bewilders the New Generation to hear of such things. Should we describe the teeth and their function, they are appalled. Not to mention the art of relieving oneself on the can—a sorrowful redundancy, or so they suppose.)

Such conversations are brief and they happen so rarely! Once there was an anomalous obstruction in the path and we were brought to a precipitous halt unexpectedly. I collided into the person in front of me—a tremendous shock, you can well imagine, to the system. We were fenced in on each side by the bright titanium tussocks so favored by the highway authorities. I could see she was distressed by the number of knicks and pocks on surfaces she had thought impervious to time and the vicissitudes of space. It was eerie not to feel the wind of forward motion. For some reason, I was impelled to speak—an old habit that reveals the extent of my dotage. I only wished to—as we used to say— "crack a joke" when I suggested we get a coffee and relax while waiting for the system to be repaired. This offended her; the New Generation is mysteriously ashamed not to have a mouth, a tongue or teeth. I should have stopped there, but something— and I admit this was perverse, criminally so—prodded me on.

There were once so many palpable pleasures, I conveyed to her with our ever more restricted vocabulary. *I wish, I dearly wish, you had a pair of lips so that I could kiss you.*

She was a bright cobalt blue, but when she blushed—a thing beyond my wildest expectations—she turned violet, a color she had surely never seen. *It is a pity and a shame* I continued, moved beyond belief, that you are so fiercely serrated. *In another time and place I might have cooked you dinner and after we might have eagerly embraced.*

This was madness on my part. I knew such talk would cause my jaws to seize up within minutes and, quite possibly, cause her to fatally percolate. Already something very like steam was spilling from her post acoustical ducts. We were bombarded by bright clusters of echoing forms, a spillage precipitated by the unexpected obstruction and the ensuing exquisite collision. With something of the old delight I noted that the concave mirrors of her eyes reflected both the tussocks and the sky above us.

I wish, I confided, *we could taste each other*!

She darkened further and condensed. To my surprise I could now behold her many aspects simultaneously. My own eyes—so unaccustomed to exereise—selected favorite objects and guessed the lovely disarray quickening beneath her dusky shell. Between the dazzling planets of her breasts her heart twinkled. *Your beauty* I conveyed to her, *is a force and . . . an atmosphere*!

At that precise instant the obstacle dissolved. Had I been able to use my nose, this dissolution would have been accompanied by the smell of burnt toast. Stillness invites reflection and its familiar subversions. Now that we were moving, the world was shut away. Already the *emblematic* encounter (I am, I admit, what was once called a Romantic) and the memory of that encounter eluded me.

Imagine rocks and raked sand—but *tinned*, as in the past sardines were tinned in oil—and you will have some idea as to the nature of my thinking once we were under way again.

La Goulue in Retirement

Once La Goulue got old and fat, *ces messieurs* no longer risked losing their hats for a glimpse of her *chatte* although only instants before, or so it seems, so many had leaned precariously close to the stage. How many silk hats has she sent soaring above the dressed supper tables and later, after her own supper, how many times has she seen a trouser fly hastily unbuttoned and a cock, its dressed head as violet as her own deep vulva, greet her with a wink? How many cocks leaping into her *chatte* as through a hoop of fire? The bright jewels tossed at her feet, the crisp violet cash rolled like cigars and pressed to her palm. Her armoires brimming with bright slippers sewn of glazed leather.

But now La Goulue is old and fat. To make a go of it, she has sold her plates, her knives and bracelets, the red petticoats and the bloomers slit so that when one kicks off a hat, one's *chatte* may size up the clientele. She has bought a weary tribe of misused animals as long in tooth as is she, and their cages and a gypsy wagon, its planking in need of paint—and where we now sit.

The animals—one bear, four lions, a black panther and a hyena—she keeps in her yard, just outside the old walls of Paris. At night she can hear the heart of Paris beating without her. She knows that those who loved her are themselves retired or in the last throes of an affair with a girl whose eye-catching beauty can do nothing to stop the pocket watch set out upon the bedside table mocking the moments as they pass. And she recalls how when she ordered duck at the Maison Dorée, the carver—and he was dressed like a bridegroom—would debone it for her, and serve the flesh in sixty perfect slices arranged like a fan. On a plate of fine faience, she tells me, painted with the green figures of Chinamen, and other curious things. The duck's fresh blood in a pewter pitcher to keep it from clotting, and stirred into the sauce. Cherries on fire, tumbling after.

The animals' food she makes with stale bread she haggles for, using what remains of her charm. The beasts, she reminds the bakers, the restaurant cooks, the neighbors—are like us. They must eat! (She does not give them bones to gum for fear of rousing old appetites; her beasts' nostalgia for better days, is as great as her own.) Every afternoon when she returns to her little scruffy yard and its cages, its piles of straw—one clean, one very dirty—her sack rattles with stale baguettes.

Her lions have all lost their teeth, as has the poor bear who, like his mistress, can no longer stir a crowd. But the panther . . . now that's another story.

On tour in the early spring, the panther had torn off a child's arm. The boy leaning far too close to the cage, wanting to *pet the kitty*. La Goulue wiggles her bare fingers in my face. She has sold the last of her rings to pay the surgeon's fees. "It is fortunate," she tells me, "the child is not a girl. Ladies love to soothe a man who has suffered such misadventures whereas *ces messieurs* will settle for nothing less than perfect beauty." I nod and accept the cup of verbena she offers along with a slice of toast thickly frosted with her own quince jam. "The cat's meat man," she sighs, "comes for the panther tomorrow."

If on a winter's morning you elect to spend time with La Goulue, she makes you feel at home. I, for one, have always been susceptible to the nostalgia of others. Her hospitality, her vivacity, her full bosom bring to mind the great aunt or grandmother one adored, whose infrequent visits were enlivened by indiscretions and gifts of tinned sweets. To tell the truth, the afternoon I spent with her, those brief, sweet moments, have left an odd impression, for looking back I see myself as a boy of ten or so and this not just because of her tales and her toast, but the fact that she presses stereoviews upon me, views of herself strolling the gardens of Versailles in a dress of the palest lavender, and again, in that same dress, standing among the fountains of St. Petersburg. And there is another hand-tinted view of the dancer in her prime, slender in camisole and drawers, straddling one of the bronze lions that guard the Spanish throne.

"You see how I was fated for lions from the start," she laughs, and squeezes my wrist as though I were a favorite nephew. And she tells me how the waiter at the Maison Dorée debones her duck in a trice, how the dwarf Lautrec entertains her and her friends with an erotic patter so hilarious it is all she can do to keep herself from pissing on her velvet chair.

"For you see," she continues, "in those brief years, appetite ruled our lives. My *chatte* kept Paris hot and lively, whereas now even my lions are geriatric, the hyena too irritable to roll over and offer her belly for a scratch, the panther doomed. My yard," she smiles sadly, "reeks of feral creatures in idleness." And she yawns. She is wanting her nap.

As we walk towards the front gate, she pulls her stiff underwear piece by piece from the line and says philosophically:

"Don't worry about me, *Monsieur*. You see: it is only natural for meteors to fall from the sky."

When I leave La Goulue—and it is late in the day—the first winter thunderstorm strikes just as I reach the street. The rainy season is fairly set in Paris, and thunder, lightning and heavy storms are common both night and day. When after midnight the clouds disperse, the stars peer down through the spare foliage of the pollarded trees, and one may see the ardent face of the moon as volatile as smoke.

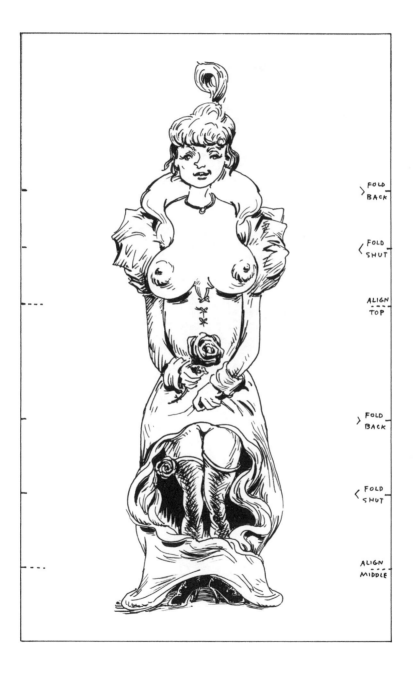

FOLD
BACK

FOLD
SHUT

ALIGN
TOP

FOLD
BACK

FOLD
SHUT

ALIGN
MIDDLE

ALIGN
MIDDLE

FOLD
SHUT

FOLD
BACK

ALIGN
BOTTOM

FOLD
SHUT

FOLD
BACK

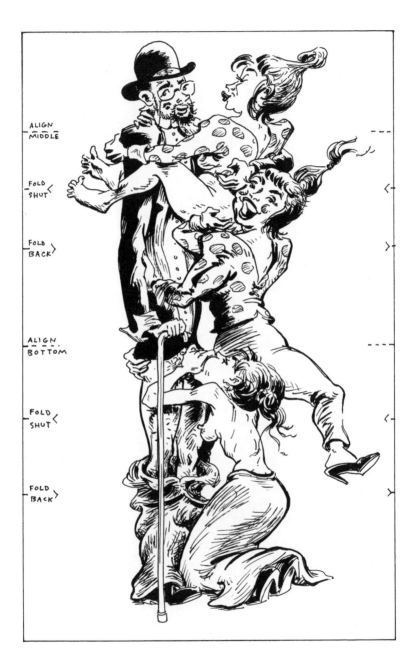

Now that the Management runs the planet, it is necessary to petition the Ultimate Authority should one contemplate deviating, however imperceptibly, from The Way. As Charles Charles is always swamped by the demands of Immediacy—the inevitabilities of which were revealed to him in the middle of the night by an ear-splitting screech—it is impossible to petition Him except in person. However, it is rumored that he might be caught off guard in the High Head at noon examining His teeth and tongue with all the attention due His rank.

On one occasion only has a petitioner managed to hide out in the High Head—and this despite the microhootered faucets. Although it cannot happen, the petitioner had crawled across the ceiling, circumventing whoopers and gongs. He had hopped from sink to sink, taking care to desensitize the eight soap dispensers—one dispenser for each of the Eight Overseers who, as it is established in The Way, soldier at the sink side by side after relieving themselves in the eight corporate cans.

The Ultimate Can is situated at the bow, as it were, of the Corporate Head, and is visible from the standpoint of the Overseers who have only to roll their sixteen eyes to the left to assure themselves of the One's corporality—surely their function's greatest advantage.

It is confirmed that the petitioner survived the rigors of the Corporate Head and miraculously penetrated (understand that I use these words cautiously and ironically) the Oval Office where he spent the night sprawled on the High Table, and this despite a blizzard of virtual asps that must surely have murderously plagued him. When in the morning the Usher flung the portals aside and Charles Charles stood poised on the threshold, his armor bleeping, his pale eyes popping, the petitioner stood before him naked and bleeding.

Charles Charles is the only one alive with firsthand knowledge of The Event. Yet it may well be that the One who is gently hammered into our collective mind as we sleep, is not the Charles Charles we thought we knew, but another, more ineffable Charles Charles. (The Eight who had stood in our leader's wake, stapled to their boots and bleating, have all been re-wired and retired.)

It is established that the petitioner wanted to be allowed to grow lettuces on the lip of his one window. This is not exactly forbidden, yet suggests treason. Why the lettuces mattered so much, why the petitioner was willing to risk everything for them, is a matter none of us is willing to drop. Indeed, we risk as much talking about those lettuces, although not one of us has ever seen or tasted lettuce. Yet we relish the rare references to them in the forbidden books, those books with the images that sear our eyes and cause our bellies to complain, as or so we imagine, the wild creatures that once roamed the outlawed wilderness, complained. Images of chargers piled high with victuals, or so we suppose, like nothing we have ever tasted. For The Way insists we eat smooth pap, untextured—but for that brief tip of the hat to roughage, which, we have been told, we must not scorn if we are to fully function.

The petitioner's teeth and tongue—considered by some as objects of horror, and by others of hilarity (and by still others as sacred relics to be referred to only cryptically) are on display in the front hall of the public refectory. When I was a small child, they were introduced to me by my father in guise of a warning or, perhaps, inspired by a premonition. Because the petitioner's persistent remains, and the constant reminder of his heresy have, over a brief lifetime of reflection, inspired me to petition in turn. I, too, would grow lettuces and, as in the Old Days, eat them with those storied condiments: vinegar and oil.

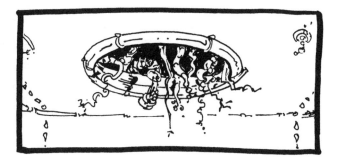

Oops!

Eek! The terrible stepdaughters! How they roar! With what disdain do they spit their food back into the plate! Poor things, they are driven—well, aren't they?—by the mother's rage. The mother whose anger soaks every single household item with the scent of scorching. The entire house reeks of fire. The new woman opens all the windows and doors and still . . . The stench! Of the mother, scorned.

And the three stepdaughters: 13, 14, 15. Each one as sinuous as a pole dancer! They bring their own smells to supper, their pots of hot tar, of vinegar and piss. Three months into the arrangement and already she corrodes. The cause of All Family Ills, she is reduced to harlotry. Like her hairy tale, her cunt refuses to stay neatly tucked away. Somehow her cunt is always there! It burns brightly like a lamp above the dinner table, illumining their dreadful repasts.

Lonely in her kitchen, her claws ill equipped for the setting of the table, the mashing of potatoes, she cooks white food for the brats, things they will swallow should they be of a mind. Lonely are her mornings, afternoons and evenings. There is no way around it: the brats' dad is riddled with debt: alimony, child support, the saving up for the prestigious college educations. One will go into Marketing, one into Finance and one, the *ar-*

tiste, can go to hell for all she cares. Is it surprising that their dad has lost his luster?

On a Saturday night he takes her out to dinner in acknowledgement of her sacrifice. The waitress, crisp as a new pickle, catches his eye. And unaware that the new husband's pockets are as thin as his frayed temper, she—O the slut!—drops a spoon beside his chair in order to retrieve it and so present her perfect arse to him, lusciously globed: *there it is*! Toasty as the planet Jupiter it balances for one stunning instant right under his nose! And that's that! This is how it comes around! The waitress' cunt supersedes her own! It glows above the table where they sit, sinners face to face, already mortally fatigued with one another.

Because His Youth
or The Parrot's Spanish

e has always depended on his boundless, one might say *uncanny*, vitality to keep his head above water. Because his youth sustains him, he cannot grow old without it. His hands, once so elegant, are now reduced to paws. His entire body like some great damaged paw. Already he can see it fallen to the pavement, its contours marked with chalk. An hour does not pass without his cursing the Fate of Man. His own fate in particular. When he sups, he sups on clay.

At lunchtime he had passed his daughter in the street. She introduced him to a raven-haired beauty in vermillion sandals who treated him to instinctive apathy. The memory of that, the girl's impeccable feet, her scent of freshly steamed rice, compounds his torment.

These days any disagreeable encounter, even with lesser creatures such as salesgirls, mortifies him. He takes care to shop in familiar places where he is respected and well known. In the precipitously receding, yet palpable past, he had purchased a Panama hat from a woman his daughter's age and with whom he flirted so successfully she called the house—the risks of his duplicity are immense—*just wondering*, she had whispered, her voice pleasantly unhinged, *just wondering if . . .*

But already unlike his former self, he had put her off. His prostate, for god's sake, gave him pause. His marvelous sperm was thicker now, unfamiliarly so—as if he had changed species. And he has! He is become a member of an endangered species.

"You are fascinating," he had said to her, wondering as he spoke how many such as she he had possessed. But his past was littered with conquests and he had lost count. "Fascinating . . ." he breathed it, "but I am about to go on vacation with my wife." He sighed and when the salesgirl laughed knowingly, he laughed along although the wife in question was relatively new and a hottie with a mane of magenta hair and a lapis lazuli navel stud. She was a successful therapist; he took wives who were independent: an actress, a scholar, a neurologist—the better to conceal his own mysteries.

"We'll leave it to your return," the girl offered with all the cheek of youth, "but when you wear the Panama, think of me."

•

He liked to say that to assess a woman's erotic capacities was a form of ecstatic divination. His clairvoyance, the ease of his seductions, establish him in his own eyes as a prince of erotic practice. And the many brief encounters, the extended affairs, demand ingenuity and diligence, a cautious crafting of the hours. (He had once loved to sail and had prided himself on his skills with charts and compass; he handled his daily agenda with equal caution.)

The women assured that he never had time on his hands—a thing he abhorred above all else. As his wives faded into insignificance, the women in their variety provided for fresh forms and a sense that his life—in fact mundane—was significant. The world carried little meaning for him, and the women functioned as semaphores. When he fucked he was alive among the living. When he fucked he was hatched of his shell like any new thing.

•

Weeks passed and when he did not call, the salesgirl wondered if, in fact, they had been laughing together at his easy duplicity and the promise it implied, or if she had simply been jacked around.

She called again. She was bored and she was broke; she wanted an older man to treat her to a good dinner at the very least. She imagined receiving presents. She entertained this fantasy: they would meet at Victoria's Secret when his wife was out of town and he would look on with admiration as she modeled underwear. She did not know that he was too much a narcissist to consider spending time and money on a shop girl. A few hours of illicit sex was all he planned to give her, although illicit sex was a thing he liked above all to give himself. Also, he was putting money aside for retirement and dental work—those inevitable indecencies. (There was a brief period when he did enjoy helping out a certain very pretty Vietnamese waitress whose exoticism and infant daughter—so full of promise—inspired unprecedented acts of selflessness.)

•

The salesgirl was his first and last experience with Viagra. Initially impressed, she soon became dubious, even skeptical. An hour into it she wondered what was wrong with him. Was he overcome with guilt, unable to forget his wife and so incapable of orgasm? Something of a sexual athlete herself, she grew irritated. And he, exhausted, looked at this woman who was gasping with irritation beneath him and for the first time in a lifetime of fucking, feared for his sanity. Fucking the shop girl was like fucking in the underworld, airless and interminable. He imagined he was an old bull about to be sacrificed to a bankrupt god; he imagined his throat was about to be cut. Hers was the last Panama he'd buy.

That night as he slept beside his wife he awakened from a nightmare, shouting.

•

In his recent youth, a mere decade or so ago, and at the height of his powers, he was a magnificent animal with an uncanny capacity to shimmer with sexual heat whenever he entered a crowded room. He thought of himself as a minotaur, his world mazed with cunts. But now he can feel himself cooling down. He considers fish oil and a personal trainer. Terrible thoughts come to him at his most intimate moments—when flossing his teeth or sitting on the can. These physical acts remind him of death, stampeding. His mood is abrasive, the minutes pernicious, his guts tied in knots. Advancing age is torture! Torture! It is like having one's knuckles fractured with screws! He thinks of the photographs taken at Abu Graib—those unfathomable mortifications. He thinks his own predicament is somehow this terrible. Hell. He might as well be shitting fossils. Pissing thorns! Like the codgers he despises precariously nursing their old bones down the sidewalk, he, too, is reduced to taking powders in order to function like a normal human being. In other words, it is evident that old age is a monstrosity of nature. There is no room left on the planet for a man trundling towards seventy at twenty miles an hour! If only he had the sexual energy he'd lost just yesterday, he'd go out like a fire-cracker. He'd go up in flames! Fuck his wife's solicitous blow jobs; fuck his doctor's cautious inquiries! Fuck his wife's twenty years' leg up on him!

•

One early evening he finds himself alone, his wife detained in city traffic. It is the end of summer and the light in the living room is dim. Another summer gone, goddammit! Even the seasons betray him. He catches himself before he can doze off. Five years more of this shit and he'll drown in his own bloody tears.

He thinks that to have lived in the present was a gift of real beauty. He thinks that those who have the gift of the present are the ones lively women like to be near. He considers that what he had offered was both indecipherable and indescribable, something manic but not exactly scary: his own brand of super attenuated joy. Unsustainable, clearly. Risky—god how it had *cost* him! But absolutely essential.

And irresistible. Not only to women, but small children, girls above all (!); sometimes little boys. When on the rare occasion he would accompany a wife to the supermarket, a little boy might offer him a gumball or a rubber worm. His current wife likes to tell how she had seen an unknown toddler dash down the canned soup aisle to hug her husband's knees. Other people's household pets adore him. Cats that habitually despise visitors leap onto his lap. Once when they walked into a café together in Merida, a dejected parrot surged to life, pressing its face against the bars of its cage to cry out with such passion all conversation stilled and everyone turned to look. And although he had only just assured his wife he would not abandon her in public places in his quest for attention—a thing that had begun to seriously test her temper—he responded to the parrot's solicitation without hesitation. His Panama balanced jauntily on a head of hair that at the time was barely threaded with grey, he walked to the cage and leaned close. The parrot's little black tongue, its eager eye and urgency caused his pulse to quicken. If the attention was anomalous and uncanny, it was also flattering. As his wife stood by impatiently tapping her foot, her bottom appealing to the local crowd, he engaged the parrot with impudent good humor. The parrot's Spanish was far more extensive than his own, yet this did not appear to faze either of them. They kept it up, his wife remarked, beyond the bounds of sense or decency.

Chi Gong

for S.F.

Once ejected from her module, Chi Gong set forth to find complex systems. Our defeated expectation is manifest in her report:

—Primates wear their pearls between their lips, whereas oysters conceal theirs beneath their tongues. Birds lay their pearls in their beards. The female of the hairless ape wears her pearl but a finger's length from her anus.

—Whereas birds sit on their beards, some apes wear theirs on their heads or between their legs. Mussels use their beards to grasp the underside of submarines.

—Although they produce shit, all terrestrial creatures—bearded or bald—are ephemeral.

—On earth, species hierarchies are not readily discernible. Absurdity—the inevitable outcome of scatological systems—rules to lethal effect. Such drear redundancies darken the entire galaxy.

—Earth is cacophonous and bile has sullied its waters. Battles are fought in God's name over beards and the length of the earlobe—God, Earth's lesser archon, whose cipher is bloody flux, and whom we, in our wisdom, have repudiated.

The Butcher's Comics

Clean

TEXT BY RIKKI DUCORNET
DRAWINGS BY T. MOTLEY

Dogs are dirty
Birds are filthy .

Fish are clean except
for the intestines
which are dirty.

People love to wash and
that's why in the eyes
of Jesus they are best.

Dogs don't go
to heaven,
they turn into
worms, but
good Christian
people stay
just the same,
younger and
smelling
good all
the time

All the people get washed
when they die and sit
at the table of
Holy Lightning
with Jesus
eating all
that
clean food.

Jesus smiles when he sees the
people washing. He knows that the
people like to be clean and that's
why he likes them better than the
animals who eat any crap dirty.

clean people who don't smell like vinegar sit at his table, only younger
with new hair, teeth and skin,

all naked but no fornicating, eating all that clean food.

that's why it's important to get the old folks soaped and combed and in to bed between sheets boiled four times and ironed into nice even creases—twelve creases for Jesus—and their toenails pared.

Our old people look good, just simple folk, the color of milk and veal roast.

When it's time, Jesus calls them, he says:

O have you pared your nails?

And they answer:

O yes Sweet Lord we have pared our nails and ironed our sheets twelve times.

and Jesus says:

Are you CLEAN?

which is a joke because he knows they are and the old folks laugh a lot at this.

And Jesus says:

Do you smell good and are you the color of roast veal?

And the old folks answer

O yes, Lord, we are clean and Our thoughts are like white sauce and our blood is like water and we are ready, O Sweet Jesus.

Then Jesus gathers them up in His arms and gives them clean teeth, the better to eat at His Holy Table, and clean ears, the better to hear his Holy Music,

—and clean eyes, the better to see and worship Him.

© 1994 DUCORNET/MOTLEY

The Tale of the Tattooed Woman

by Rikki Ducornet · ILLUSTRATED BY T. Motley

Mutilation has enhanced my beauty, and if this were an age when men worshiped marvels, they would bring more than thin coins to see me.

They would bring the rarest things they own. They would give what I would ask.

I would ask for particles of flesh.

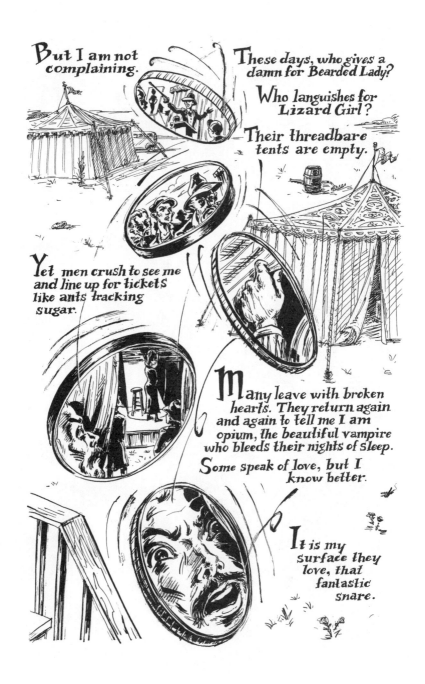

But I am not complaining.

These days, who gives a damn for Bearded Lady?

Who languishes for Lizard Girl?

Their threadbare tents are empty.

Yet men crush to see me and line up for tickets like ants tracking sugar.

Many leave with broken hearts. They return again and again to tell me I am opium, the beautiful vampire who bleeds their nights of sleep.

Some speak of love, but I know better.

It is my surface they love, that fantastic snare.

If they saw me as you do, they would hide their tails and run.

For I am hateful.

You see that.

You have never been taken in, not even for a moment, and from the first perceived the truth.

Years ago, you asked me how it began. You have been patient, and strangely enough, unafraid. This has endeared you to me.

Today I will tell you my story.

I was born a twin.

The effort killed my mother. And the other, a bloated, lopsided thing, also died.

I took a breath and screamed. I screamed for seven years.

I was never still. When toads or scarabs fell into my hands, I tore them to shreds...

...and looked on laughing when ants carried the gritty droplets of ordure to their clotted cellars.

Everything angered me. My dolls, their waxy faces and china hands, my bland picture books and animals of ivory.

145

My father gave me a canary. In a tantrum I bit off its head.

Despairing, he threatened to lock me away forever so that this world of creatures and things would be safe.

For a time I carried my hatred sheathed like a dagger within me.

Life was peaceful. Roses grew in the garden. I consumed my rice and milk and no longer trampled my dresses to shreds.

I took naps. I was good. So good that for Christmas my father gave me that greatest of gifts—trust— in the shape of a flat-nosed pug of such high race it could barely breathe.

A stupid animal, it loved me dearly. it slept at the foot of my bed. For hours each night I caressed its thick neck, feeling the life throb there.

Then one day I coaxed it into a trap that the gardener had set for a vixen. I watched it bleed to death. The beast's agony flooded my heart with delight.

Fear came after. And the terrible knowledge that my appetite for destruction was insatiable. With a pen from my father's study and stolen ink, I pressed a mark beneath my skin, a blue tattoo on my wrist to remind me NEVER TO KILL AGAIN.

And here it is, a black seed lost in a forest, the molecular center of a diminutive rose. And the rose is one blossom in a garland of blossoms, leaves, and purple thorns that circle my wrist, very like those at my ankles and throat.

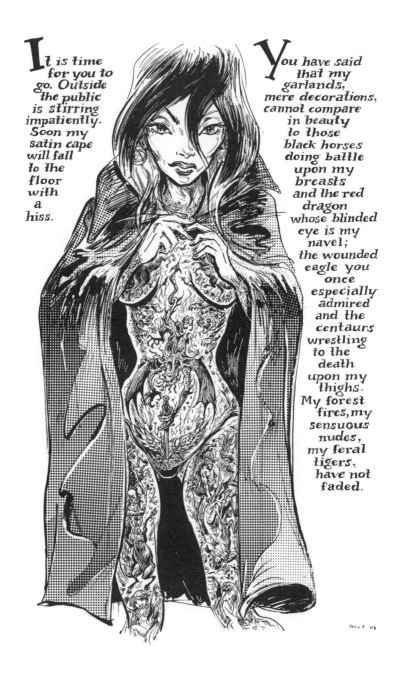

It is time for you to go. Outside the public is stirring impatiently. Soon my satin cape will fall to the floor with a hiss.

You have said that my garlands, mere decorations, cannot compare in beauty to those black horses doing battle upon my breasts and the red dragon whose blinded eye is my navel; the wounded eagle you once especially admired and the centaurs wrestling to the death upon my thighs. My forest fires, my sensuous nudes, my feral tigers, have not faded.

BRILLIG

by Rikki Ducornet

adapted by T. Motley

When the poison had come in the form of treason as foreseen in the prognostications of the Perfect

...the Jumblies, having survived a punitive somersault through alien space...

...founded Outpost number One,...

...Upon the only habitable island of the Thousand Thousand.

The Thousand Thousand fluctuate in a perpetual state of inexplicable process. The planet's GEOGRAPHY SCRAMBLES. the star is notoriously inhospitable. Its living organisms decline and extinguish with hair raising celerity

1.

The **Outpost** was built in what the **Jumblies** named Sector Seventy-Seven of the Thousand Thousand.

But because sectors burglarize from one another, all definitions are tenuous.

The Outpost periodically loses members and parts.

These materialize elsewhere.

2.

According to oral tradition, hard edges were perceived for the first time during an instantaneous drought.

Horizons took on the comforting definitions of **flagstaffs and steeples.**

Once these had been invested with the powerful names of the **Old Gods,**

Those unutterable names that give permanence and protection,

They vanished.

The drought transformed **Brillig** into a tangle of combustible trash the Jumblies feared would ignite in the heat of starlight, ending their miserable sojourn in conflagration.

Instead, chameleons materialized in the rubbish with outsized eyes that spun in their heads like wheels.

3.

They could not be eaten, nor could the *future* be retrieved from their bowels, as they had none.

They brought to mind an ancient narrative — something to do with flintboxes and enchantment. To PUNISH himself for not having had the **perspicacity** to commit this tale to memory, the Perfect, swearing by the PURITY of his inner vehicles, MORTIFIED his testicles WITH tHORNs.

4.

It was in this parched season that the Jumblies dragged forth the first **Eggs**.

The Perfect warned that the Egg was **taboo** as the unborn, unblemished by **Time**, are sacred. The more heretical insisted that the gift of **Eggs** proved that **Fate** was looking after them still, and that rather than quibble, the **Perfect** should himself partake of the feast. He refused and was left to jabber on his mat.

Not long after he was found dead, his throat slit from ear to ear in the ceremonial manner.

5.

That night the JUMBLIES tied themselves to trees for fear of being swept to deadlier zones.

They watched in impotent horror as the Eggs gave way to dragons with the faces of owls.

6.

Deep in their heart of hearts the Jumblies wondered why Gods once generous had now chosen to torture them. Was this the price of spacegreed? Would they ever again know Order and Plenitude — ideals they had worshiped on aching knees in the pronged temples of their lost world?

Briefly I will describe the Jumblies:

their heads are green and their hands are blue; they are naked and bad-tempered;

their babies are born blemished by a shocking growth of black hair recalling the tufted epaulettes of senescent subtropical terrestrial baboons.

some Jumblies have tails.

we may have seen snouts.

They are all short, they snort, they dribble, they argue nonsense, they venerate spotted beans; above all they goggle alarmingly at visitors. These brutes are no more vessels of Light, but cages of Night bolted shut by by the savage demands of this, the darkest of planets.

8.

The Jumblies have come to cherish their harrowing existence.

They could not tell us how long they have been marooned;
each and every one of them hotly insists he is the
descendant of an extinct species of shellfish.

Had their stunted memories been sharper, still they
could not have told us much: time is figured loosely
in epochs named for the planet's shiftless moods
and the evil spells of its seasons.

9.

Of their starship nothing remains. Mud-colored jellyfish vegetate in the ooze where she crashed; only glass has withstood this swindle called a climate.

The Jumblies have used her established orderings of copper to coronate their Perfect, yet say the CROWN is the gift of Figurant Archons from a drug-induced dream.

The Jumblies dream abundantly and from that other nebulous star HAVE brought back the MANY squalid practices that typify Brilligeois' culture — including a method for keeping the cult eggs intact by soaking them in quicksand boiled in urine. To each his owl-faced dragon; the Jumblies choose to preserve, hatch, else SMASH his own — unhatcHED to bits, at PUBERTy.

The Jumblies looked upon us WITH hostility. When the questionable surface upon WHICH we had teleported BEGAN to fumble WITH OUR cellular interpreters (and some feared with our minds) we departed.

The Jumblies and their Perfect could not know that we were responsible for the seeding of BRILLIG with their precarious lives...

...and yet, as we rose IN A puff of smoke, they turned their scowling faces to the sky and shook their fists.

11.

We abandoned the abject formlessness of BRILLIG in time to see a wall of MUCK sweep across the overhang upon which we had stood, instants before, cringing in the gloom.

A skeptic among us has BEEN converted to the FAITH;

the visit to BrilliG has convinced him...

13.

that THE entire physical universe
is an INVENTION of DEMONS.

SELECTED DALKEY ARCHIVE PAPERBACKS

Petros Abatzoglou, *What Does Mrs. Freeman Want?*
Pierre Albert-Birot, *Grabinoulor.*
Yuz Aleshkovsky, *Kangaroo.*
Felipe Alfau, *Chromos.*
  Locos.
Ivan Ângelo, *The Celebration.*
  The Tower of Glass.
David Antin, *Talking.*
António Lobo Antunes, *Knowledge of Hell.*
Alain Arias-Misson, *Theatre of Incest.*
John Ashbery and James Schuyler, *A Nest of Ninnies.*
Djuna Barnes, *Ladies Almanack.*
  Ryder.
John Barth, *LETTERS.*
  Sabbatical.
Donald Barthelme, *The King.*
  Paradise.
Svetislav Basara, *Chinese Letter.*
Mark Binelli, *Sacco and Vanzetti Must Die!*
Andrei Bitov, *Pushkin House.*
Louis Paul Boon, *Chapel Road.*
  Summer in Termuren.
Roger Boylan, *Killoyle.*
Ignácio de Loyola Brandão, *Teeth under the Sun.*
  Zero.
Bonnie Bremser, *Troia: Mexican Memoirs.*
Christine Brooke-Rose, *Amalgamemnon.*
Brigid Brophy, *In Transit.*
Meredith Brosnan, *Mr. Dynamite.*
Gerald L. Bruns,
  Modern Poetry and the Idea of Language.
Evgeny Bunimovich and J. Kates, eds.,
  Contemporary Russian Poetry: An Anthology.
Gabrielle Burton, *Heartbreak Hotel.*
Michel Butor, *Degrees.*
  Mobile.
  Portrait of the Artist as a Young Ape.
G. Cabrera Infante, *Infante's Inferno.*
  Three Trapped Tigers.
Julieta Campos, *The Fear of Losing Eurydice.*
Anne Carson, *Eros the Bittersweet.*
Camilo José Cela, *Christ versus Arizona.*
  The Family of Pascual Duarte.
  The Hive.
Louis-Ferdinand Céline, *Castle to Castle.*
  Conversations with Professor Y.
  London Bridge.
  North.
  Rigadoon.
Hugo Charteris, *The Tide Is Right.*
Jerome Charyn, *The Tar Baby.*
Marc Cholodenko, *Mordechai Schamz.*
Emily Holmes Coleman, *The Shutter of Snow.*
Robert Coover, *A Night at the Movies.*
Stanley Crawford, *Log of the S.S. The Mrs Unguentine.*
  Some Instructions to My Wife.
Robert Creeley, *Collected Prose.*
René Crevel, *Putting My Foot in It.*
Ralph Cusack, *Cadenza.*
Susan Daitch, *L.C.*
  Storytown.
Nicholas Delbanco, *The Count of Concord.*
Nigel Dennis, *Cards of Identity.*
Peter Dimock,
  A Short Rhetoric for Leaving the Family.
Ariel Dorfman, *Konfidenz.*
Coleman Dowell, *The Houses of Children.*
  Island People.
  Too Much Flesh and Jabez.
Arkadii Dragomoshchenko, *Dust.*
Rikki Ducornet, *The Complete Butcher's Tales.*
  The Fountains of Neptune.
  The Jade Cabinet.
  The One Marvelous Thing.
  Phosphor in Dreamland.
  The Stain.
  The Word "Desire."
William Eastlake, *The Bamboo Bed.*
  Castle Keep.
  Lyric of the Circle Heart.
Jean Echenoz, *Chopin's Move.*
Stanley Elkin, *A Bad Man.*
  Boswell: A Modern Comedy.
  Criers and Kibitzers, Kibitzers and Criers.
  The Dick Gibson Show.
  The Franchiser.
  George Mills.
  The Living End.
  The MacGuffin.
  The Magic Kingdom.
  Mrs. Ted Bliss.
  The Rabbi of Lud.
  Van Gogh's Room at Arles.
Annie Ernaux, *Cleaned Out.*

Lauren Fairbanks, *Muzzle Thyself.*
  Sister Carrie.
Leslie A. Fiedler, *Love and Death in the American Novel.*
Gustave Flaubert, *Bouvard and Pécuchet.*
Kass Fleisher, *Talking out of School.*
Ford Madox Ford, *The March of Literature.*
Jon Fosse, *Melancholy.*
Max Frisch, *I'm Not Stiller.*
  Man in the Holocene.
Carlos Fuentes, *Christopher Unborn.*
  Distant Relations.
  Terra Nostra.
  Where the Air Is Clear.
Janice Galloway, *Foreign Parts.*
  The Trick Is to Keep Breathing.
William H. Gass, *Cartesian Sonata and Other Novellas.*
  A Temple of Texts.
  The Tunnel.
  Willie Masters' Lonesome Wife.
Etienne Gilson, *The Arts of the Beautiful.*
  Forms and Substances in the Arts.
C. S. Giscombe, *Giscome Road.*
  Here.
  Prairie Style.
Douglas Glover, *Bad News of the Heart.*
  The Enamoured Knight.
Witold Gombrowicz, *A Kind of Testament.*
Karen Elizabeth Gordon, *The Red Shoes.*
Georgi Gospodinov, *Natural Novel.*
Juan Goytisolo, *Count Julian.*
  Makbara.
  Marks of Identity.
Patrick Grainville, *The Cave of Heaven.*
Henry Green, *Blindness.*
  Concluding.
  Doting.
  Nothing.
Jiří Gruša, *The Questionnaire.*
Gabriel Gudding, *Rhode Island Notebook.*
John Hawkes, *Whistlejacket.*
Aidan Higgins, *A Bestiary.*
  Bornholm Night-Ferry.
  Flotsam and Jetsam.
  Langrishe, Go Down.
  Scenes from a Receding Past.
  Windy Arbours.
Aldous Huxley, *Antic Hay.*
  Crome Yellow.
  Point Counter Point.
  Those Barren Leaves.
  Time Must Have a Stop.
Mikhail Iossel and Jeff Parker, eds., *Amerika:*
  Contemporary Russian Writers View the United States.
Gert Jonke, *Geometric Regional Novel.*
  Homage to Czerny.
Jacques Jouet, *Mountain R.*
Hugh Kenner, *The Counterfeiters.*
  Flaubert, Joyce and Beckett: The Stoic Comedians.
  Joyce's Voices.
Danilo Kiš, *Garden, Ashes.*
  A Tomb for Boris Davidovich.
Anita Konkka, *A Fool's Paradise.*
George Konrád, *The City Builder.*
Tadeusz Konwicki, *A Minor Apocalypse.*
  The Polish Complex.
Menis Koumandareas, *Koula.*
Elaine Kraf, *The Princess of 72nd Street.*
Jim Krusoe, *Iceland.*
Ewa Kuryluk, *Century 21.*
Eric Laurrent, *Do Not Touch.*
Violette Leduc, *La Bâtarde.*
Deborah Levy, *Billy and Girl.*
  Pillow Talk in Europe and Other Places.
José Lezama Lima, *Paradiso.*
Rosa Liksom, *Dark Paradise.*
Osman Lins, *Avalovara.*
  The Queen of the Prisons of Greece.
Alf Mac Lochlainn, *The Corpus in the Library.*
  Out of Focus.
Ron Loewinsohn, *Magnetic Field(s).*
Brian Lynch, *The Winner of Sorrow.*
D. Keith Mano, *Take Five.*
Micheline Aharonian Marcom, *The Mirror in the Well.*
Ben Marcus, *The Age of Wire and String.*
Wallace Markfield, *Teitlebaum's Window.*
  To an Early Grave.
David Markson, *Reader's Block.*
  Springer's Progress.
  Wittgenstein's Mistress.
Carole Maso, *AVA.*
Ladislav Matejka and Krystyna Pomorska, eds.,
  Readings in Russian Poetics: Formalist and
  Structuralist Views.

HARRY MATHEWS, *The Case of the Persevering Maltese: Collected Essays.*
Cigarettes.
The Conversions.
The Human Country: New and Collected Stories.
The Journalist.
My Life in CIA.
Singular Pleasures.
The Sinking of the Odradek Stadium.
Tlooth.
20 Lines a Day.
ROBERT L. MCLAUGHLIN, ED.,
Innovations: An Anthology of Modern &
Contemporary Fiction.
HERMAN MELVILLE, *The Confidence-Man.*
AMANDA MICHALOPOULOU, *I'd Like.*
STEVEN MILLHAUSER, *The Barnum Museum.*
In the Penny Arcade.
RALPH J. MILLS, JR., *Essays on Poetry.*
OLIVE MOORE, *Spleen.*
NICHOLAS MOSLEY, *Accident.*
Assassins.
Catastrophe Practice.
Children of Darkness and Light.
Experience and Religion.
The Hesperides Tree.
Hopeful Monsters.
Imago Bird.
Impossible Object.
Inventing God.
Judith.
Look at the Dark.
Natalie Natalia.
Serpent.
Time at War.
The Uses of Slime Mould: Essays of Four Decades.
WARREN MOTTE,
Fables of the Novel: French Fiction since 1990.
Fiction Now: The French Novel in the 21st Century.
Oulipo: A Primer of Potential Literature.
YVES NAVARRE, *Our Share of Time.*
Sweet Tooth.
DOROTHY NELSON, *In Night's City.*
Tar and Feathers.
WILFRIDO D. NOLLEDO, *But for the Lovers.*
FLANN O'BRIEN, *At Swim-Two-Birds.*
At War.
The Best of Myles.
The Dalkey Archive.
Further Cuttings.
The Hard Life.
The Poor Mouth.
The Third Policeman.
CLAUDE OLLIER, *The Mise-en-Scène.*
PATRIK OUŘEDNÍK, *Europeana.*
FERNANDO DEL PASO, *Palinuro of Mexico.*
ROBERT PINGET, *The Inquisitory.*
Mahu or The Material.
Trio.
RAYMOND QUENEAU, *The Last Days.*
Odile.
Pierrot Mon Ami.
Saint Glinglin.
ANN QUIN, *Berg.*
Passages.
Three.
Tripticks.
ISHMAEL REED, *The Free-Lance Pallbearers.*
The Last Days of Louisiana Red.
Reckless Eyeballing.
The Terrible Threes.
The Terrible Twos.
Yellow Back Radio Broke-Down.
JEAN RICARDOU, *Place Names.*
RAINER MARIA RILKE,
The Notebooks of Malte Laurids Brigge.
JULIÁN RÍOS, *Larva: A Midsummer Night's Babel.*
Poundemonium.
AUGUSTO ROA BASTOS, *I the Supreme.*
OLIVIER ROLIN, *Hotel Crystal.*
JACQUES ROUBAUD, *The Great Fire of London.*
Hortense in Exile.
Hortense Is Abducted.
The Plurality of Worlds of Lewis.
The Princess Hoppy.
The Form of a City Changes Faster, Alas,
Than the Human Heart.
Some Thing Black.
LEON S. ROUDIEZ, *French Fiction Revisited.*

W. M. SPACKMAN, *The Complete Fiction.*
GERTRUDE STEIN, *Lucy Church Amiably.*
The Making of Americans.
A Novel of Thank You.
PIOTR SZEWC, *Annihilation.*
STEFAN THEMERSON, *Hobson's Island.*
The Mystery of the Sardine.
Tom Harris.
JEAN-PHILIPPE TOUSSAINT, *The Bathroom.*
Camera.
Monsieur.
Television.
DUMITRU TSEPENEAG, *Pigeon Post.*
Vain Art of the Fugue.
ESTHER TUSQUETS, *Stranded.*
DUBRAVKA UGRESIC, *Lend Me Your Character.*
Thank You for Not Reading.
MATI UNT, *Diary of a Blood Donor.*
Things in the Night.
ÁLVARO URIBE AND OLIVIA SEARS, EDS.,
The Best of Contemporary Mexican Fiction.
ELOY URROZ, *The Obstacles.*
LUISA VALENZUELA, *He Who Searches.*
PAUL VERHAEGHEN, *Omega Minor.*
MARJA-LIISA VARTIO, *The Parson's Widow.*
BORIS VIAN, *Heartsnatcher.*
AUSTRYN WAINHOUSE, *Hedyphagetica.*
PAUL WEST, *Words for a Deaf Daughter & Gala.*
CURTIS WHITE, *America's Magic Mountain.*
The Idea of Home.
Memories of My Father Watching TV.
Monstrous Possibility: An Invitation to
Literary Politics.
Requiem.
DIANE WILLIAMS, *Excitability: Selected Stories.*
Romancer Erector.
DOUGLAS WOOLF, *Wall to Wall.*
Ya! & John-Juan.
JAY WRIGHT, *Polynomials and Pollen.*
The Presentable Art of Reading Absence.
PHILIP WYLIE, *Generation of Vipers.*
MARGUERITE YOUNG, *Angel in the Forest.*
Miss MacIntosh, My Darling.
REYOUNG, *Unbabbling.*
ZORAN ŽIVKOVIĆ, *Hidden Camera.*
LOUIS ZUKOFSKY, *Collected Fiction.*
SCOTT ZWIREN, *God Head.*

FOR A FULL LIST OF PUBLICATIONS, VISIT:
www.dalkeyarchive.com